Also by María Ospina

Variations on the Body: Stories

Only a Little While Here

a novel

María Ospina

Translated by Heather Cleary

Scribner
New York   Amsterdam/Antwerp   London
Toronto   Sydney/Melbourne   New Delhi

Scribner
An Imprint of Simon & Schuster, LLC
1230 Avenue of the Americas
New York, NY 10020

No amount of this book may be reproduced or stored in any format, nor may it be uploaded to any website, database, language-learning model, or other repository, retrieval, or artificial intelligence system without express permission. All rights reserved. Inquiries may be directed to Simon & Schuster, 1230 Avenue of the Americas, New York, NY 10020 or permissions@simonandschuster.com.

This book is a work of fiction. Any references to historical events, real people, or real places are used fictitiously. Other names, characters, places, and events are products of the author's imagination, and any resemblance to actual events or places or persons, living or dead, is entirely coincidental.

Copyright © 2023 by María Ospina Pizano
English language translation copyright © 2026 by Heather Cleary
Published in agreement with Casanovas & Lynch Literary Agency S.L.
Originally published in Colombia in 2023 by Penguin Random House Grupo Editorial, S. A. S. as *Solo un poco aquí*

All rights reserved, including the right to reproduce this book or portions thereof in any form whatsoever. For information, address Scribner Subsidiary Rights Department, 1230 Avenue of the Americas, New York, NY 10020.

First Scribner hardcover edition March 2026

SCRIBNER and design are registered trademarks of Simon & Schuster, LLC

Simon & Schuster strongly believes in freedom of expression and stands against censorship in all its forms. For more information, visit BooksBelong.com.

For information about special discounts for bulk purchases, please contact Simon & Schuster Special Sales at 1-866-506-1949 or business@simonandschuster.com.

The Simon & Schuster Speakers Bureau can bring authors to your live event. For more information or to book an event, contact the Simon & Schuster Speakers Bureau at 1-866-248-3049 or visit our website at www.simonspeakers.com.

Manufactured in the United States of America

10 9 8 7 6 5 4 3 2 1

Library of Congress Cataloging-in-Publication Data is available.

ISBN 978-1-6680-9708-3
ISBN 978-1-6680-9710-6 (ebook)

 Let's stay in touch! Scan here to get book recommendations, exclusive offers, and more delivered to your inbox.

For Eleazar and all his creatures.
For the dogs who have welcomed me since I was a girl.
For the scarlet tanager I hope is still alive.

Only a Little While Here

Do we truly live rooted in earth?
Not forever on earth:
only a little while here.
Even jade crumbles,
even gold cracks,
even quetzal feathers turn to dust.
Not forever on earth:
only a little while here.

> —Nezahualcoyotl, fifteenth century

To arrive in a state of leaving. Zepquasqua

> —Anonymous,
> *Dictionary and Grammar of the Chibcha Language*,
> early seventeenth century

To split
is always to split in two.

> —Cristina Peri Rossi,
> "The Journey," tr. Arthur Malcolm Dixon

Monkeys, moose, cows, dogs, butterflies, buffaloes.
What we would give to have the ruined lives of animals
tell a human story—when our lives are in themselves
the story of animals.

> —Ocean Vuong, *On Earth We're Briefly Gorgeous*

I

The Colloquy of the Bitches

Wherever you go, I must follow.
Ep-quaque va vm nangaxin, vm suhucas inanga.

> —Anonymous,
> *Concise Grammar of the Mosca Language* (c. 1612)

What I have heard lauded and praised is our remarkable memory, our gratitude, and great fidelity, so that we are often painted as symbols of friendship; and you'll have seen, if you have looked, that on alabaster tombs with figures of those buried there, when they are husband and wife, between the two, at their feet, the figure of a dog is placed as a sign that in life their friendship and fidelity were inviolable.

> (Cipión, a dog, to his friend Berganza, another dog)
> —Miguel de Cervantes,
> *The Colloquy of the Dogs*, tr. Edith Grossman

And on that summer street,
that hidden street,
she dropped a petal of her life
and went on her way.

> —Homero Expósito,
> "The Orange Blossom"

I used to have two Dogs. They kept close watch to make sure everything was divided fairly—food, petting, privileges. Animals have a very strong sense of justice. I remember the look in their eyes whenever I did something wrong, whenever I scolded them unfairly or failed to keep my word. They'd gaze at me with such awful grief, as if they simply couldn't understand how I could have broken the sacred law. They taught me quite basic, plain and simple justice.

> —Olga Tokarczuk,
> *Drive Your Plow Over the Bones of the Dead*,
> tr. Antonia Lloyd-Jones

Kati

Kati cocks her head, perks her ears, and sharpens her hearing as she always does when trying to decipher a mystery.

"Go home, my pretty mutt!" Luis gives his command with the gruff love he usually shows her as two men in uniforms lift him by the arms and his legs swing wildly in the air.

She cranes her neck the other way and starts barking again. He should know she's home already, though they only came to live in this park a few days ago. Perhaps she wonders if he's talking about the alley from before, the one from which they were removed in the middle of the night, along with all the others who were run off with firehoses and tear gas.

His shouts as the men drag him toward the van only seem to enrage her more, and she joins in the tumult with rasping howls that fill her mouth with foam. She makes a lunge for one of them but stops short to avoid his kick.

"Be safe, my Kati. Wait for me at home and I'll see you there soon," the captive pleads as they haul him into the back of a van sputtering blue light across the pavement. "I'll be right back, girl, I promise. Go home!"

Maybe Kati can't hear him after the men close the doors. She runs toward the machine as it grinds into motion to take him away. She gallops behind it for two blocks, as if trying to stop it with her fury, as if she were utterly certain her barking could smash it to pieces. She doesn't seem to know what to do with her anger when she realizes she's lost the race. She manages to dodge a motorcycle that nearly runs her over in the middle of the street, then keeps barking from the solitary sidewalk. Perhaps what shoots from her raised hackles is rage. Perhaps all her desire to bite someone gathers in her back teeth. She growls and no one bears witness. No one is left to notice her in those small hours when streets downtown are practically deserted.

Even as she lets out a few of the angry barks still boiling inside her, she seems to remember the man's command and his promise. She returns to the park that is their home now, near the trunk of a young guayacán where late at night he stations his cart, stretches out a tarp, and builds the cardboard shelter where the two of them will curl up under the covers to fight exhaustion and cold.

Kati tucks her paws under her and nestles into the blankets, as if trying to cling to the warmth he managed to spread over them before being dragged away. This time she doesn't sleep, though she might be tired after her usual nocturnal prowling. She is panting, but perhaps not to cool down. She keeps one eye on the corner where last she saw him, as if not wanting to miss the moment he gets back. Several men return from working and plant their carts nearby—more people who had needed to flee late that other night when uniformed men came with their tanks and their hoses meant for destroying homes. She seems to recognize them. And also the woman who always arrives around that time to set up her arepas stand in front of the motel that never closes. Maybe Kati catches the scent of melted cheese and burned butter. Maybe she likes it. Amid the dust, the hoarse machinery of tumbledown buses announces the nearing daybreak. As the scent of light rain and diaphanous clouds brushing the ground blooms, she finds refuge farther under the cart without ever taking her eyes off the corner where the man and his promise disappeared.

She has known how to defend their home from thieves since she was young. How to watch over the cartons and cans, the blankets, the radio and bags of bread, the bottles of water, the box where he saves leftovers for her, the rubber boots and raincoat for when it pours, the tools and length of rope, the giant sacks of recycling and the tarps that some construction workers gave them recently. She knows how to raise her hackles, how to peel back her whiskered lips to reveal her fangs, how to bark loud enough to intimidate anyone. This time, though, she doesn't need to bite. Two guys circling the cart head the other way when they notice her vigilance. Later, the white dog limps over to say hello. A longtime friend and neighbor who just moved into the park, like her. They eagerly smell each other's creases and rub their fur together, as if trying to narrate with skin and fibers the events of a night's pilgrimage across cement. Seeing him seems to comfort her somewhat. He might even sense the substance and vibration at the root of her disquiet.

Midmorning, with frantic muzzle, Kati tears into the bag where Luis keeps the food he collects from restaurants or stores and devours the hodgepodge inside. There's no water in her dish, so she goes looking for puddles nearby. She drinks from a well that has formed on a slide in the playground and then trots back to the cart, not wanting to be away from it for too long. The shops along the street are open by then, and the sounds of traffic mingle with the shouts of street vendors in the park pleading for someone, anyone, to buy their avocados, peach palm fruits, padlocks, phone chargers, and slippers for cheap.

At sunset, when fewer people pass by and the mountain falls dark, the men from the park begin to leave with their carts. Kati perches her front paws on hers, which Luis should be pushing, to rummage through the bags until she finds a few slices of bread that she might recognize are not meant for her. Perhaps the stillness of that evening strikes her as odd, since it is when they would normally begin their adventures. Back in the blanket she dozes off, half-opening her eyes each time some dissonance breaks the mechanical murmur of metal and horns and the music still radiating from certain doors. Every so often, she drags her eyes toward the corner where he disappeared, maybe hoping he's about to return. But the only thing she detects all night is a dog sniffing through the trash scattered across the sidewalk, four men who return to park the carts they've filled, and a few people coming and going from the motel. Perhaps she misses feeling the commotion of the streets through the soft pads of her paws, or the joy of rifling through the garbage that the city offers on every corner at nightfall. Or maybe she longs for something else entirely.

As the morning settles in, Kati gives herself a shake and goes for a walk, maybe out of hunger because she can't find anything else to eat in the cart. If he were to see her, he would notice right away that her pluck and the determination of her gait have faded, that hesitation has seeped in between her ribs and has turned her cadence clumsy. If he were to see her, he would notice the tension in her nose, which hardens and dries with illness or misfortune.

Kati earns two chicken bones when she peeks into the lunch spot across from the park where Luis usually asks for scraps to give her. On any other day, she would have waited until she got back to the cart to pick them clean slowly, but this time she tears into them right there on the sidewalk with all the zeal of her molars. Then she turns the corner in the same direction as always, toward the mountains that interrupt the tangle of streets and walls through which they would usually shuffle together. This time, she doesn't stop to scratch with pleasure the way she often does on this or that corner when she is with him. She is looking for scraps left on the sidewalk after the garbage truck passes, but others have gotten to them first.

"Kati!"

She runs excitedly to the woman sweeping the corner and bows her head to sniff the bag placed on the ground for her, then swallows with voracious enthusiasm the bones and rice that the woman has brought her from home. When she finishes, she sticks her nose in the bag again, as if pleading for it to be full again.

"So hungry today I don't even get a hello? Come over here, come say hi like the good girl you are."

The street sweeper gives her shiny back a scratch and she licks the woman's worn glove.

"Footloose and fancy free these days, are we?"

Kati wags her tail and lodges herself between the legs of the woman petting her.

"What a pretty girl you are, and sweet as always. Where'd you leave your papito this time? You tell Luis to drag his lazy bones down here now and then, I haven't seen him for days!"

The woman's caresses seem to cheer her a bit.

Kati continues on her way to the square she usually visits with him in the afternoons. She knows how to sit on the corner by the Palacio de Justicia like he taught her when she was little and to wait while he disappears down the streets around the cathedral, certain he will honor his "be right back." She knows how to settle in behind the sign he places on the sidewalk, how to guard the plate where the coins fall and stay put until he returns with their cart full of cans and boxes to congratulate her on a job well done. Today, however, this quotidian combustion is interrupted by tumult: a wall of jumping, whistling, screaming people block her usual path across the square.

"Fund schools not war!"

"Education is a human right!"

Perhaps the vibrations of the drums filter upward through the pads of Kati's paws. She seems confused by the whistles and shouts emerging from hundreds of mouths at once. Maybe she hopes, just for a moment, that he's somewhere in the raucous crowd, though she might have no idea where to start looking. She slips between the legs of the throng, trying not to get stepped or jumped on, desperately tracking an exit from this forest of frantic limbs. Her muzzle hard at work, she sniffs each leg she encounters, perhaps with the idea of finding him among the rebellious bodies shaking the square.

"People over profits! Don't treat us students like terrorists!"

Atop the shit-covered statue of Simón Bolívar, the pigeons Kati loves to chase have been replaced by several bodies waving flags. Dodging kicks and shoves, she makes her way across to a clearing near the cathedral and runs into a line of riot police bulging against the plastic and dark metal wrapped around them. Who knows if she is surprised by the fact that instead of faces, they have large helmets that reflect the unruly crowd and the storm clouds above. Perhaps she senses the arrogance that seeps through the gaps in their uniforms. Maybe she remembers that it was men like these who cast them from the street where they had always lived. She seems to curse them with each bark. Until a kick from behind knocks her away. No one hears her terse yelp. No one notices as she runs terrified along Carrera Séptima, against the throngs, dodging the crowds still arriving with furies different from her own to fill the square, despite the tear gas.

Kati scrapes the walls with her side, as if begging for shelter until she manages to escape down the first street where Luis always collects bales of cardboard and paper and tosses them in their cart. The street they usually take on their way back home—to the old one or the new one, it doesn't matter because they aren't far apart. She shakes off several times, as if trying to rid herself of the human grease left on her coat, then returns to her light, determined gait, as if she had no time to cower under the police officer's blow. She untucks her tail. When she stops in front of the building occupied for months by several Emberá families, she doesn't find the leftovers they always leave for her near the rubber tree that bursts through the cement.

She deftly avoids the buses and cars stuck along the avenue that borders the park. She might note the presence of their empty cart. But this time she continues on, crossing at the next street, perhaps because she intuits that he's waiting for her in their previous dwelling, the place where they had always lived. Until they were exiled. The new emptiness of the street must surprise her as she nears the alleys that surrounded her former home. Perhaps she is surprised by the rancid smell of dust, stronger now than ever. She stops and urinates beside a huge sign that reads:

> Coming Soon:
> New Arts District
> Building a Better Bogotá!

Kati trots under the yellow tape that keeps pedestrians from entering and slips through a small gap in the wall of blue tarps that now covers the alley where she grew up. Sharpening her gaze, she lets her muzzle trace heaps of ochre earth and the clouds of dust kicked up by machines that claw at the few dilapidated buildings that remain. She looks for a place to take shelter from the dredgers and cranes diligently pushing matter around, carving through unclaimed walls and windows, and zealously demolishing roofs, then lopes across this lot condemned to vacancy toward the rubble piled where her home used to be. She stops twice to lick a toe pad cut open by a shard of metal. Struggles her way up the ruins and finds a plank to lie down on. Surveys the vast dispossession. If he were to see her, he would understand that grief seems also to reside within her defiant blinking.

It is too late when, anxious, she turns to see who is creeping up on her from behind. Two masked men slip a cord around her neck. She growls and bucks, trying to counter their tugs, but they win the duel.

"Female. Easy, girl. Easy. No one's going to hurt you."

She folds backward, frantic, in search of the loop that traps her. The pads of her paws scrape against splinters of glass and wood when she resists being dragged toward a van. Despite the cord that chokes her and makes her cough, she manages to spit out a few furious growls that likely convey the ire that has been fermenting in her for days. Who knows if hers is the last rage to echo in that wasteland. (Later, far from there, she will release different furies and seek different shelter, but she doesn't know this yet.) Three cats caged inside the van join her with their yowls as the men dodge Kati's snapping teeth, slip a muzzle on her, lift her into the back, and close the doors.

Mona

"You stay here like a good girl. Someone will take you home, you'll see."

When she sees the woman who has always given her orders get into the car and close the door, Mona tries to pull free from the leash that binds her to a fence. She erupts in frantic barking as the car disappears into traffic, but her cries are absorbed by the afternoon's revelry. Two women eating at an outdoor café nearby get annoyed and move to another table. In the lush park at the other end of the street, voices rumble from a pair of speakers and a crowd gathers around a giant screen to watch a soccer match.

At the end of a taut leash, Mona alternates between whining and panting. She seems exasperated, choked by questions. She sniffs each body that passes her on the sidewalk, keenly aware of everyone leaving the café, and eyes each car that stops nearby. Perhaps she is clinging to the hope that they'll return for her. As the shouts from the group watching the soccer match swell, her howls seem to reveal the collapse of her last remaining certainties.

When the crowd disperses and cold begins to slide down the mountain, Mona finally lies down. Who knows if her rapid panting reveals her waning patience, though like any good apartment dog, she has been waiting since she was born. She observes as her surroundings slowly grow dark and notices when the cafés and restaurants turn off their lights and the patio beside her empties. Watches two men take down the giant screen and remove it from the park. Ignores the sounds of traffic, which are starting to die down. Intones a thin, maybe inquisitive, whimper from time to time. She no longer seems convinced anyone can hear her, as if she were beginning to resign herself to a certain absence.

The last person to leave the café approaches her.

"What are you doing here so late? Where did your owner go?"

Mona stands quickly and warily tries to get a sense of the woman who is locking the café door and scanning the street for someone she doesn't see. The dog timidly sniffs the hand offered to her muzzle as a test of her docility and then retreats.

"Who left you here? Has it been long?"

Mona watches the woman walk away and then stop for a moment.

"Don't worry, someone will come for you soon."

She continues to follow the woman with her eyes as she walks down the street, turns back twice more, and then disappears around the corner. Mona lies down against the wall again, gathering her body and folding her front paws under her to combat the nighttime cold that has begun to lick insistently at her coat.

From where she is stationed, waiting, she glimpses a pair of women who dig through the trash and collect the cans left around by visitors to the park. She watches three men enter nearby buildings for their shifts as security guards, and others who have just gotten off work and are walking away. Sometimes she closes her eyes, but who knows if she is able to rest. Worry seems to interrupt her sleep. Maybe she had never really heard the tumult of thrushes and sparrows before that dawn, accustomed as she'd been since birth to mornings in the padded enclosure of a house with carpets and a front door. As it gets lighter, with the same dedication she showed as a puppy rebelling against her restraints, she begins to chew on the leash that binds her to the fence. She works at the nylon cord with her strong molars until she has gnawed her way through.

Once free, she gives herself a shake to slough the dew from her coat and crosses the street into the still-empty park. She urinates on a bed of lilies of the Nile. Goes in search of water in the cups left on the grass. Licks the crumbs from a package of food she finds under the swings and sniffs her way around the trees, though this time without the excited curiosity she used to carry on her back, that insatiable desire to spend hours deciphering the annals of the soil. This time, she is not run through by the exaltation she would feel whenever they took her for a walk through the park in her neighborhood, even though this is the first time she is loose on the grass. After a while, she returns to wait at the fence where her tattered leash still hangs.

"And what are you still doing out here on the street?"

The woman from the night before returns when the clamor of the morning has settled and the mountain's mist has dissipated and been forgotten. Mona must recognize her, because she approaches with her tail relaxed, as if welcoming her.

"Poor girl. They have no right to do this to you."

Mona lets the woman pat her side and remove the piece of leash that still hangs from her neck, marking her orphanhood. Who knows if she can sense the pain and guilt braided through the woman's chest ever since she had to abandon her own dog fourteen years earlier, when she started getting death threats and had to flee her town for Bogotá. Mona watches her enter the café, open the windows that face the street, sweep, and set up tables on the patio. She voraciously accepts two hard pieces of pan de yuca and drinks from the bowl of water the woman brings out to her.

Sometimes Mona sits. Sometimes she lies down. She inspects everyone who ignores her on their way into the café, though she occasionally interrupts her investigation to observe a satisfied dog joined by a leash to a person as they walk past. Maybe she feels the weight of her empty stomach when the scent of breads and meats being consumed outside neighboring restaurants slips into her nose. Maybe these smells mix with the soaps and perfumes emanating from the bodies of other passersby. Who knows if any of those floral auras remind her of the ones applied each morning by the woman who abandoned her. She crosses the congested street a couple of times to sniff recent traces left in the park and takes a shit next to a freshly planted flowerbed, ignoring the dogs walking leisurely with their owners and smelling the world from the comfort of full bellies and companionship, the way she used to do. She dodges the advances of a young boy who chases her after escaping from the bench where his nanny had tried to make him sit. In different times, she would have offered her brown back to be pet, but she doesn't seem inclined to give of herself so readily anymore. Instead, she anxiously devours a few chicken bones left behind by construction workers on their lunch break. She always returns to her fence, as if only beside that dusty border can she imagine them returning for her.

The woman from the café appears again as night falls. Mona swallows the old bread she leaves on the ground in just a few mouthfuls and arches her rib cage against the woman's leg, accepting her caresses.

"Now why did they leave you here all alone like this?"

Mona wags her tail shyly and accepts the cardboard that the woman has placed on the ground for her to sit.

"Let's see what we can do tomorrow if they haven't come for you by then. Don't worry, we'll figure this out. They're probably on their way already, just be patient."

Mona licks the woman's mottled hands when she reaches down to scratch her chest.

"You just stay there like a good girl."

Of what substance is woven the force that binds her to that threshold, preventing her from following the woman as she disappears down the street? Mona nods off on her new bed until rain begins to pool around her muzzle. She walks to a nearby store, where she finds an awning that shields the pavement. Maybe it is surprise that makes her bark at the pale bodies posing paralyzed in bikinis on the other side of the glass. But she soon appears to grow used to her stiff company because she lies down on her side right there on the cement and falls asleep. She gets up when the skies open and a puddle begins to soak her elbows and moves to the corridor of the old building next door. The night watchman shines his flashlight at her through the glass, but, determined to settle in somewhere, she ignores him and lies down against the wall as soon as he walks away.

When the sun comes up, she is awoken by a woman who has come to clean the building.

"Scram! Get on home and don't you come back! Dirtying up my doorway."

Mona leaves, perhaps frightened by the umbrella the woman is shaking at her. She crosses the park in search of food but finds nothing. Maybe the hunger rattling around her insides unsettles her. She urinates and returns to the same fence, where her cardboard has been destroyed by the rain, and drinks some water from a bowl filled by the downpour before lying down on the damp mat in front of the café's entrance. She licks her paws, something she has enjoyed ever since she was little.

"How are you still here? What are we going to do with you?"

Mona devours the plate of rice and the bone the woman from the café has brought her from home. She wags her tail as she watches her lay out a sheet of plastic and some newspaper beside the fence, then follows her to the door, as if asking to go inside.

"You can't come in, love, I'm so sorry but they won't let me. Wait out here on your new bed like a good girl, I'll think of something. I'm sorry."

Mona stands for a while on the other side of the glass. Her ears prick up. She seems to be studying her reflection, which might appear different to her than it did in the huge bathroom mirror in the only home she's ever had. (Not until years later, far from there, will she live in an apartment again and see herself reflected again in a surface that smooth.) Her tail droops, as if disappointed, then something—maybe resignation or exhaustion, maybe both—sends her back to the newspapers that soften the wet cement. She scrutinizes every person who passes her on the sidewalk or enters the café on that morning heavy with clouds. Each car door slamming shut sends a jolt through her. Whoever came across her there would see privation and sorrow in her eyes.

At noon, when the woman steps outside again to visit her, Mona lies on her back and offers her neck to be rubbed, as if begging her to seal a pact of affection.

"I know you're sad. What a terrible thing to do. How could anyone abandon you like this?"

The woman kneels beside her and lets her fingers wriggle down to Mona's spotted belly. The dog keeps her eyes on the horizon while her powerful paw bounces against the woman's arm, perhaps asking her never to stop. Who knows if she is reminded of the boy she used to live with, who would rub her belly just like that, grazing her soft nipples that will never give milk. She is startled by a gentle tug at her throat.

"Come with me, sweet girl. It's for your own good. Get up and walk now, that's a good girl."

Mona lets herself be led by the woman's rope but seems to hesitate, as if some old loyalty were holding her back. A man helps the woman lift her into the trunk of a hatchback. Maybe she's surprised to be carried, accustomed as she was to jumping into the car of the woman who lived with her until a few days ago. Perhaps she is relieved at the prospect of leaving that soaking wet street full of suspicions because, even though she tucks her tail between her legs, she doesn't protest. Does she think they're taking her home? Or does she have her doubts?

"It's going to be okay, hear me? You're a brave girl and I know someone's going to love you. I mean, it's not that I don't . . . Everything will be fine, you'll see."

Perhaps Mona hears her voice crack as she says this. The woman tells her to lie down before she closes the door, but Mona remains standing, though her long legs fit clumsily inside the small trunk. Who knows if questions bubble up inside her as she stares at the woman waving to her from the other side of the glass. A *How could this be possible* or a *Where's the home they promised was mine*. A *Who is this man* or an *Am I being abducted or saved*. And, if so, where do these questions dwell? Mona jumps at the trumpets and kettledrums of the salsa music that bursts from the speakers when the ignition turns over. No one in the street hears the sharp bark she lets out when she realizes she's being taken away.

Canine 127 (Young Female / Spayed / Vaccinated / De-Wormed / Microchipped) —Lady
Canine 128 (Young Female / Spayed / Vaccinated / De-Wormed / Microchipped) —Reina

Kati is the first to wake when the metal door's distant clang announces that someone has arrived. Mona groggily opens her eyes; she does not seem pleased that the other has peeled herself so abruptly from her side and slipped from between her paws, disrupting the warm ball that preserves their heat in the small hours of the morning. Kati slides her muzzle between the bars of their kennel, and Mona approaches her lazily after watching her join the ruckus of the other dogs in their cages. Neither can see the people whose voices reach them from the far end of the hall but maybe, despite the smell of disinfectant, cement, and mildew, they can sense that their usual caretaker is coming and that he is bringing new people with him. The two puppies in the opposite cage watch them quizzically and bark in shrill little chirps, as if trying to emulate them.

They must recognize the voice of the man who adores them. He's getting closer. Mona whines in anticipation and spins in a tight circle. When he stops in front of their cell, they wag their tails furiously.

"Good morning, beautiful girls."

Whimpering desperately, the two rise on their hind legs to rest their paws high on the grating. Perhaps they know it's not time to eat because they haven't been let out in the courtyard yet. They seem completely disinterested in the strange man holding hands with a little boy. Despite their danced pleas for affection, their caretaker turns away from them and faces the puppies.

He explains that they're the youngest dogs in the shelter, that they were picked up a few weeks ago and should be around four months old now. That they're ready for adoption.

"They look like good breeds. What other young dogs do you have?"

"There's these two . . . you can see how clever and sweet they are. The black one is around two years old, and the brown one is probably closer to three or four. You can tell they had owners because they came in healthy, with good teeth and everything, and they're very well behaved. Someone trained these girls."

The caretaker sticks his fingers between the bars of Mona and Kati's cage. Between animated leaps, they jostle each other with their muzzles to get closer to his caresses. The boy copies him.

"Daddy, look how sweet! Can they come out?"

Mona licks his small fingers with her generous tongue. Kati has taken a step back and appears satisfied to decipher their flesh from a distance. The man draws the boy away from the kennel.

"We'll take a puppy, but it has to be the male. Women are such damn sneaks, I bet bitches are just the same."

The unknown man laughs to himself. The caretaker lifts the puppy from his cage and holds it up to the bars of Kati and Mona's.

"Say goodbye to everyone . . . Ladies, wish him luck!"

Mona watches them walk away with her head tilted to one side, as if trying to figure out why the man who takes care of them refused for the first time to enter their cage and play. There is a spring in her step as she heads to the back of the cell, where Kati, perhaps out of boredom, is lying down again.

Mona jumps on top of her and bites the black fur on her neck with delicate intensity. With growls that seem to be of pleasure they begin to roll around, delightedly twisting their dark bodies together, ignoring the howls that fade as the metal door clangs shut.

II

Detour in the Canopy

Bird. Sue guana. l. sue
The wing of a bird. gaca
When a bird swoops. guasamiʃqua
Birdsong. ainsuca
A cloud of birds. isua

—Anonymous, *Concise Grammar of the Mosca Language* (c. 1612)

What is it like to live among the birds?

—Aristophanes, *The Birds*

O, hummingbird!
pierce the flowers no longer,
emerald wings.
Do not be cruel.
Come down to the riverbank,
emerald wings,
and see me weeping
by the red water,
see me weeping.

—José María Arguedas, *Deep Rivers*,
tr. Frances Horning Barraclough

How do birds know
the exact moment
they can take to wing
without danger?
Which flight nerve
tells them
they are free again
among the leaves?

—Fabio Morábito, "I Hear Cars"

All above us is the touching
of strangers & parrots,
some of them human,
some of them not human.

—Aracelis Girmay, "Elegy"

He has no desire for skyscrapers; what he wants is forest. But he must be exhausted, and this time, despite the wisdom of his fibers, he does not seem to know how to find it. Nor do the others. Bewitched by the light, they swirl around the sharp tip of a building that attracts and ignores them, that flaunts its electric victory, its hunger for steel and glass, for cables and ownership, and shoots them through with its glow. The meteorological radar captures them that night in their trance, though not entirely. Thousands of restless bodies amass in the form of a vast green stain that clouds the experts' screens. Later, a distressed scientist will analyze the image and report the disaster. But the radar is not able to reveal the thrust of those, the feathers in frantic movement, the fury of wings and tail feathers flashing in the glow of that deceptive high-rise. Yellow, gray, and spotted birds; brown, red, and greenish-black ones; white, orange, and blue. Disoriented wings and weary bodies that before this trap were all purpose and thirst for their destination.

If someone were to open a window that September night, up there in the Manhattan sky (but who would do that in a climate-controlled office building where windows are for having your back to?), or if one of those ornithologists who sometimes climb to the top of the building were there to record the song of those lost birds, over the sounds of traffic she would pick up their uncommon cries, their entreaties. She would notice the clamor of their panic, their desperation to learn from others trapped in the same bright spiral why their compass is stuck, why they can't keep moving south. Where is that path charted by the stars and recalled by their sinews since before they made their first journey? Where is the route followed resolutely for thousands of years by those of their kind? If someone were to listen carefully to that dissonant clamor, she would venture that they are asking all this.

The scarlet tanager has been part of this circular flock for only the few hours since, transformed into a nocturnal long-distance flier, he left his Connecticut forest and lost track of the stars as they vanished from the sky. Now he flies like the rest toward the garish lights of the tower that call to him, seeking to draw him off course. The tanager's mother (like so many mothers here) passed through what was by then already called New York on her way south, without glass and filaments to hold her in thrall. And, of course, on her way back north. For thousands of years, his ancestors had survived predators and storms. For centuries, they watched humans shuffle around beneath them as they charted their course, bridging tree and star. Only to have it all come crashing down now.

Lost in the vortex, the tanager flies robotically—perplexed, maybe, by his own impulse—among the cluster of cramping fans goading him on. Perhaps it is the company of hundreds of other large and small birds shrieking and flapping the same detour, or perhaps it is the current of air they create with each beat of their wings forced to worship electrical light that urges him on in this orbit that equalizes them all, that melts the differences between them.

In the images transmitted by the camera installed at the top of the high-rise to offer panoramic views of New York to any curious individual online, someone might discern the rapid movement of those small bodies that interrupt the Financial District's skyline. She might mistake them for insects and conclude, as people often do, that this is all routine. No one would know with any certainty that the furious body of the scarlet tanager is one of the thousands of splotches on the venerated panorama of steel, cement, and sky. Or that all around him exhausted birds are collapsing after hours spent flying in a spiral.

When morning finally dilutes the electrical glow, two volunteers from the Bird Alliance catalog the corpses of

    warblers
    kingbirds
    troupials
    orioles
    thrushes
    vireos
    sanderlings

cuckoos

flycatchers

and other tanagers

that have plummeted 110 stories to the pavement of Fulton Street.

By that time, the doorman in charge of the main entry to the skyscraper will have finished his shift and will be stepping outside to find the fallen birds, confirming the fear that plagues him each spring and fall. As on recent mornings, he will be troubled by the bodies that carpet the street with their recently deflated chests, with the vital mist of their breath still dissolving in the dawn. He feels a stab of rage as he observes on the asphalt the silence of wings that once lived to defend the air. He is afflicted by all those aborted journeys, by the painful peace of inert flesh that once was millimetric pulses distilled into dance.

He knows, because he was raised by a grandmother who taught him to find in that north the flocks she saw as a girl in Tennessee, that birds are majesty and good omen. To honor them, and to soften his grief, he has been giving them funerals. As he does whenever he finds such a massacre on the pavement, he will scoop as many little bodies as his large hands allow into his backpack and carry them the hour and a half it takes to reach his apartment in the Bronx by subway. He and his daughter will bury them in the corner of a nearby park, under the shade of a cedar far from the path, near other graves they dug in the spring and the autumn before. The little girl will make a cross of sticks for each one and will sing a song she made up, during the last burial season, to say goodbye. She has begun to intuit that, even in death, these bodies that lived to defy gravity are company to her. That autumn, she will begin to understand what her father has told her: that eyes, hearts, muscles, and feathers will one day mix with cosmic dust to become foliage and berries and roots. That everything the city tries to pave over, those layers of dirt and clay that appear beneath the cement when the electrical company's machines punch holes in the street, is star and tumult, tendon and blood and flight. The trace of countless movements. And she will feel a bit less like a little girl, a bit more lost and less inclined to believe that the world is made of games and sweets.

An ornithologist who studies the migration of endangered birds will notice on his computer screen that morning a strange detour in the journey begun a week prior in Vermont by a cerulean warbler he has been tracking for two years. The tiny sensor—complete with geolocator, accelerometer, magnetometer, and thermometer, which he attached to the soft blue of the bird's back in order to discern the exact path of its journeys to and from South America—will report a series of unusual movements near the southern tip of Manhattan, then a slow return north. The device, which must have survived the impact that extinguished the bird's intentions, will be transmitting its signal from a park in the Bronx. The scientist will arrive a few days later and, searching for his treasured warbler, will stumble upon the small crosses in little mounds of dirt that mark the improvised cemetery. Unearthing several birds, he will dig until he finds the geolocator still clinging to the blue-winged body and limp neck into which worms have begun to bore. He will notice the glimmer lingering on the regal white breast of the animal he believes to be his. He will never know who buried her there, or why, and it will be hard for him to accept that the small bird he chose to accompany from a distance in her travels from north to south to north to south to north along the continent could now be a corpse mourned by others. That someone else could claim her, someone who knows nothing of routes, hormones, conservation status, or extinction risk. Someone who has no idea how hard the creature was to catch and tag. He momentarily considers staying at the warbler's tomb to interrogate the undertaker when he returns. But he will decide against fighting over bones. He will take the decomposing bird, sensor still attached, with him in a sterile bag along with two other warblers he finds buried nearby, though not before returning the rest of the flock to their eternal beds.

When the bereaved scientist freezes the cerulean warbler's cadaver in his laboratory, he will pluck a few of her white and blue feathers to keep in a glass box on his nightstand. He will have no way of knowing, as he analyzes the sensor's data from those days, that for a few hours a scarlet tanager flew close to his bird, brushing against her feathers, perhaps. That the blackwing passed beside the bluewing warbler and the two were joined in a longing for south and in songs of confusion and fury before one of them died.

Fervent, the tanager manages to save himself from that darkness. He circles the incandescent building, completely in its thrall. Perhaps he longs for the infallible signals from his flesh that in other autumns led him south, avoiding this trap. As dawn thins the tower's electric glow, the maelstrom of birds that have withstood this ordeal of flight dissipates, as if the survivors had discovered the door of a cage they had been searching for hours to find. The tanager too exits this captivity, to face its effects. Perhaps he is distressed by the twitching of his muscles. Maybe thirst cracks his tongue and exhaustion cramps his tail. Trying not to crash to the ground, he pauses on the sill of a nearby window. He seems to waver. He has saved himself from crumbling onto a Manhattan sidewalk carpeted with chicken bones and melted gum, roiling with hurried, bunioned feet. But this is probably not how he sees his salvation. Perhaps he does not recognize himself in the scraggy and disheveled yellow, reddish, and black feathers he sees reflected in the glass. He rests there for a moment, stunned, as if waiting for his heart to slow a little and for the numbness to abate. The metal below his feet sparkles in the morning light. Finally, he can close his eyes.

Something may have withered in him during this detour, but it is not his devotion to foliage. Battling fatigue, he flies toward a few trees that present themselves atop a lower building. On this hotel rooftop adorned with decorative plants and chairs for sunbathing, a security camera films him as he lands on a hedge and drinks water from a small fountain. It will not capture his movements in the bushes when he breakfasts on a beetle and two moths, nor when the veil of his eyelids drops. The video recording of the bird will live in a database that houses files from hundreds of cameras owned by the security company. It will be deleted one year later without ever being viewed.

In his previous journeys, the tanager had always been able to cover a tremendous distance on the first night. Now, however, having just emerged from the chaos, the vigor of his wings seems disconnected from his flesh. Perhaps standing on a branch on that terrace for a while will bring them back into harmony. It will be weeks before he reaches his cloud forest. Who knows how much the lost night concerns him. Or how he is pierced by the passage of time, which for him might be a tangle of altitude and stars we will never understand. Or something else entirely.

*

At 10:17 p.m., the radar at Dulles International Airport in Washington announces the presence of hundreds of birds flying southeast. The tanager is among them, though no one will be able to discern with any precision his body plump with brio or his frantic wings burnishing the air. From the tower, the technician on duty first notices the orange blotch on the screen, then later confirms the animals' appearance on the monitor of the infrared system designed to warn of all kinds of flying objects. She confirms that the airspace incursion alarm is about to sound and studies the pulses collected by the radar to determine that what will be bursting into the air corridor in a few minutes are birds, rather than monarch butterflies or bats or moths. Range: 1700 to 2500 feet. Size: varied. She sends the alert report to air traffic control, thinking that it is, after all, the middle of September; she is pleased that, though her back hurts every day from spending her life in front of those monitors, thanks to her no one ever crosses the flight path of anyone else—or at least almost never. She can see on another screen that all takeoffs and landings have been suspended for ten minutes and that air traffic control has set new altitudes for the planes in the air, and is run through by the same relief that frolics between her ribs when the heroes of the shows she watches with her boyfriend every weekend escape danger in jungles and deserts. There is nothing more satisfying than a body rescued from the perils of being in the wrong place at the wrong time.

But then she feels the sorrow that swells in her throat each time the vast flocks appear and she needs to send out an alert. The pang she tries to ignore but that has overwhelmed her since she took this job last spring identifying winged bodies in Dulles International's airspace, despite the good salary and health insurance. She is tormented by something about the furious beating of their wings, though their journey is translated so obliquely on her screen. Their ebb and flow always make her think of her parents, now in their twenty-sixth year of forced immobility in New York after flying in from Ecuador and never getting their papers. Sitting in her imperturbable tower, helping everyone else travel through the air, she is unsettled by the gap between the movement of some and the involuntary stillness of others. The previous night (while the tanager grappled with the skyscraper twenty-three blocks from the restaurant where her father works), her mother had confessed that she didn't want to celebrate her sixtieth birthday, even though everyone was already asking her about the party.

"What do I have to celebrate? That I've been stuck in the back of a store ironing clothes for a bunch of gringos? You know I should be back in Cuenca by now, leaving flowers on my mother's grave and helping your sister with her baby girl."

And the successful daughter, who was born in the United States and could go to university there, who has a gift for identifying airborne creatures on the screens of next-generation radars meant to be read by certified technicians like herself, the daughter who gladly supports others' dreams of flying around the world, still has no idea how to console her.

*

The tanager flies with an ardor that blurs his colors; this seems less a matter of anxiety than of wisdom. He looks for dense foliage full of September crickets where he can recover from his detour. In a forest in the suburbs of Richmond, where leaves still cheat the strident death autumn will soon bring, an enormous man in camouflage sees him approach the stream where he usually sits to birdwatch. During the few seconds the man manages to capture him on the branch of a maple with his binoculars, he will notice that the bird's yellowish feathers still retain traces of the lurid red he wore during that summer's mating season. He will seem thinner than the others the colonel has seen in his four years of obsessive searching for migratory birds since he returned from Iraq and Afghanistan and retired from the army. The man is beset by the same anxiety he always feels: a burning sensation on his forehead that spreads to his temples and drives him crazy, the tiny crisis produced by the lag between seeing the bird with his eyes and finding it, or not, through the lens.

Only recently did he discover that his fascination with these birds did not stem from the colorful plumage of some, the most conspicuous of which still dazzles him, or their fiery aerial dance (he has seen huge machines slice through the air and light drones masquerading as little creatures drop bombs from up high). What stirs the sweetest disturbance in him is realizing that birds perceive things he could never even imagine. The complex songs they call each other with, songs he strains to hear after so many wartime explosions left him nearly deaf. The colors they see, which will never be his. The air he will never caress as they do (no matter how many fighter planes he has flown), the canopies they probe, the night become movement. A universe not transmittable by a soldier's infrared goggles or thermal imaging cameras or the drones he authorized on so many missions. Sometimes he is overwhelmed by the thought that he is in the same forest as they are and yet is still so far from these creatures that disregard and reign over him as they cultivate their distant breath. He curses and adores this state of agitation. He chides himself for never noticing them before he retired. He mourns the decades he spent not seeing them.

He has learned to accept that these birds erode his longstanding military faith in maps, machines, and orders. Like when he was captain of a company in Afghanistan and his binoculars or drones revealed something that didn't demand war. Women washing clothes in a village or children playing in the road. And he knew that bringing his gaze closer with a powerful lens was an easy way to see the color of their eyes, but it would never unlock the order of their lives. Though he did not confess it to anyone at the time, in the end he was grateful to have confronted the bewilderment produced in him by those bodies that did the opposite of ask for his protection. They defended their secrets, just like the birds he comes to this forest every day to see.

The tanager darts up to the crown of a mulberry tree and hides among the leaves, as if refusing to allow the man to capture his image using his new camera with its formidable lens. The man is again disappointed at not being able to press the button on the device quickly enough. All he gets is a blotchy residue left by the figure of the bird in motion. So he settles for recording the animal in his notebook of ornithological observations.

Scarlet Tanager—male
James River National Wildlife Refuge, 7:13 a.m.

When he returns home, he will make a report in an online birdwatching database that tracks flight paths and estimates the populations of species all over the continent. He will also add to the list a rose-breasted grosbeak, an eastern kingbird, and two Baltimore orioles (a name he knows does them no justice as migratory birds). He will not report any other birds he sees that day because those others don't fly such long distances or flout the borders that the politicians he usually votes for worry so much about. Those others stir no wonder in him.

As is becoming his habit, he will show his most recent bird photographs to the Guatemalan woman who has been coming to clean his house for the last six months. Sometimes he feels embarrassed by the joy that shoots through him when he shares them with her, but he hasn't wanted to figure out why. She will say "Good" because she barely speaks any English, and her tongue will get tied in knots as she tries to pronounce the names he recites to her. He will try to explain to her how he has been trying to capture a clear image of a scarlet tanager for several seasons now but hasn't been able to because they prefer the highest branches of the tallest trees, and looking up for so long hurts his neck.

She doesn't speak enough English to tell him that she too has experience with long journeys across many countries, though not by air (she has never been in a plane). On foot and by bus and on the roof of a train and in other people's trucks. She would like to confess to him, though she knows it would take forever with the online translator, that when he shows her his photos of migratory birds each week, she wonders who has faced more obstacles: her and her young son during their recent crossing into Texas, as they dodged gangs and immigration officers, or one of those beautiful animals that defy walls, rails, papers, and weapons. Nor will she mention that she nurtures her own devotion to birds. That she dearly misses the green parrot she inherited from her grandmother, who is like her sister because she grew up with her, and whom she hasn't seen since she left her with an aunt in Zacapa when she left for the United States. Or that she's worried because her aunt says the bird has fallen silent since her departure, that she sends her voice messages over Whatsapp every day so she won't die of grief. Sometimes she cries when she sees, from the window of the bus on the way home, a sign in front of a pet store advertising baby parrots on sale for three hundred dollars. But she won't tell the man this, either.

He won't think of the connection between these vastly different journeys until three autumns later, when the woman who clears the dust from his world will be gone from one moment to the next. The morning she is deported to Guatemala in the only airplane she will ever set foot in after her request for asylum is denied, the man will go to the nature preserve to examine the ebullience of the creatures making a layover in his neck of the woods. He will think of her as he and his lens wait for a bird to descend for a drink from the river. He will wonder if she was able to take the binoculars he'd passed down to her recently, or whether she left them at her sister's house with her son. He will intuit her relief at the removal of that court-ordered electronic bracelet around the lacerated skin of her ankle after months of monitoring, and that she no longer needs to run to the wall jack each time the low-battery warning starts to beep. He will speculate about the beautiful birds one might see in Guatemala and will picture an indigo bunting, which migrate to Central America at that time of year and which he has only seen online. He will promise to make the trip soon. Maybe he'll see his first quetzal and maybe, while he's there, he could stop by to see her, even though reunions always make him nervous.

*

The tanager takes off a few nights later into calm skies with a flapping of wings that is a revolt against all centers. His lightness masks effort and compulsion as he flies over failed vegetable patches where abandoned cars and mobile homes gather rust about which no one seems to care. He crosses suburbs where trees compete with poles bearing flags that announce borders he flouts as he soars over vast groupings of identical houses with mowed lawns where people have forgotten about trees altogether. Shut inside those climate-controlled mansions surrounded by pristine yards where people fantasize about conquering the foliage, exterminating all earthly insects, and the divine right of private property, very few think fondly about the creatures outside. Almost no one longs to feel leaves welcome their skin, or to investigate the patience of lichen, or to face a destiny of digging in the dirt. Very few know of the audacious birds that take over the skies for several nights each year without anyone's permission.

In North Carolina, the radar used by a team of scientists to study the effects of climate change on birds registers him along with thousands more. But it only manages to translate him into a tiny dot in a blotch invading the map like a trickle of water. Pixels that silence the enormous flock's urgent need for pilgrimage and tropics.

Coordinates: 34.68853, -78.59514

Time: 12:32 a.m.

*

In his race against the cold and dark descending on the world, the tanager might be eager to press forward, but a premonition seems to hold him back. By the morning before a hurricane arrives to churn the world, the bird has already calibrated the humidity, measured the wind that tousles the feathers of his head, and scanned the heavy clouds. When the storm breaks on the coast, rattling trees and cars and billboards and factories and rooftops and flags, the tanager is far from there, hiding from its fury with millions of other birds. Amid the deluge he finds shelter in trees that cleave the walls of an old mansion with weathered columns. Up from the foundations of the plantation home already becoming rubble, vines press, fungi spread their spores, and branches scrape victoriously at brick. The tanager crams its weary chest into an eave, in the corner not yet occupied by a woodpecker, beneath weevils tirelessly eating through the beams. Three days of fog, flooding, and sanctuary. Occasionally, he manages to eat a drowned spider. The rest of the time he can only wait, stoic, for the storm to pass.

*

When the thunder and rain abate, the tanager perches on the winds of the storm's wake to propel himself southward. Who knows how heavy his limbs feel, now that he is so thin, or whether it is hunger that stops him before dawn in a park in the city of Charleston. He dilutes his thirst in a fountain carpeted with coins and viscous mud, then soars to the top branch of an old elm that grazes the enormous column beneath the statue of the country's seventh vice president. He seems unconcerned with the furious man of bronze competing with the trees and surveilling all around from on high. He splatters the lichens wrapped around the tree's bark with his excrement and, as if catching his breath, he awaits the arrival of a morning that promises to be clear.

From that high up, he might not see or might not care about the three masked women climbing the monument to mark its pedestal. But perhaps the unfamiliar stench of the aerosol cans they empty beneath him does manage to disturb the peace of his beak, unsettling him.

Take it down!
Fuck Calhoun!
Racist statues gotta go!

Accustomed as he is to other gleams and spectra, does he manage to detect the explosion of red that the women launch at the plaque naming that infamous advocate of slavery? The camera on one of their cell phones films the whole thing from the ground but doesn't manage to capture the bird above them as he seems to reignite. It doesn't register the sway of his fibers, which seem to vacillate between the urge to sleep, to keep watch, and to consummate a desire for ants.

Startled by the police sirens that wail and interrupt the dawn with blue flashes, the tanager alights on the highest branch, as if that slight movement of his wings might help him gather momentum before deciding whether to mitigate his fatigue elsewhere. As if trying to decipher each wave that rises to his branch, he bobs his head, looks from side to side, crouches, bows, and nods, perhaps weighing the shouts of the women, who run off and the screech of the approaching patrol cars. He crosses the park to alight on a palm and looks for something to eat.

The police drone that hovers nearby once the sun has risen does not detect the tanager. Perhaps he recognizes the hum of the metallic creature flying above the tree line as a sign of danger when the blue jays begin to shriek more frantically. It has interrupted his hunt for insects. He flies over a street and several buildings to land on one of the great oaks that have lived for hundreds of years beside city hall.

In the park he left behind, an osprey will spread her wings and squawk with fury in the nest she built between the statue's bronze feet, then launch herself at the electric bird that has entered her domain without permission. She will tilt at its propellers with her hooked beak and tear at it with her claws until it crashes to the ground. Its electric tirade will end and soon all will return to its morning flutter. One block over, the tanager is probing new bark.

*

No one sees the tanager for a while. Undetected by the world's machines, he flies over countless vehicles carrying sleepless drivers along highways that interrupt glades and lakes. Houses with coiffed gardens that seem uninhabited and houses overtaken by junk. Illuminated athletic fields, empty parking lots, brief towns. Huge warehouses and small ones, factories with tall smokestacks. Vast crops of tomatoes, corn, fruit. Forests reduced to perfect rectangles. Pastures full of old equipment no one even remembers. Lots stocked with new cars waiting for owners.

There are those who might feel relieved to know that millions of migratory birds have chosen the night and not the day for their travels. That way they don't have to witness so many scars across the earth, so many airplanes sporting advertisements, so much sand stolen from its banks, so many highways where there once were rivers, so many machines rising early to rake over bones old and new. Or do they sense all this anyway, from way up there?

*

The tanager needs a forest to revive him before his inevitable sea crossing. Like thousands of other birds, he lands at the end of the peninsula in the crown of one of the legions of stubborn trees resisting arsenic, lead, and pesticides. Who knows if he feels them defy the chemicals that singe their roots and contort their drive for fractals and height. Unfamiliar with the sign that indicates poisonous runoff, the tanager will drink from puddles in the toxic mud. He must have an expert's palate for the temperaments of water and the mud that flavors it, and perhaps this time he detects unfamiliar resins and bitterness. He is no stranger to waters settled by burning sediment that may have pained his stomach or scalded another organ. Who knows if he is resigned to them.

As the tanager descends to the defiant forest beside the Homestead Temporary Shelter for Unaccompanied Children, the officer in charge of morning inspections at that prison for children who crossed what some call a border is peering at the security camera monitors. She has been put on high alert since a girl from Honduras escaped a week prior and ended up asking to be taken in at a nearby ostrich farm.

On camera one, approximately 150 boys wearing uniforms step in a line onto the soccer fields that frame tents and buildings. They prepare for their morning exercise before they are led into the hangars for the rest of the day. Four men direct the boys, who, with robotic steps, struggle against a force that seems to pull them backward. (A fan of science fiction movies, the officer imagines an electromagnetic current from another dimension working against them as they try to move forward. She considers how different these boys seem from her own son, always so eager to run around anytime a door opens.)

On camera two, some 250 girls of different ages arranged in two lines by height, wearing uniforms and orange caps. They walk along a path, marked by barricades, that leads them to the large hangar that houses the cafeteria. Ten women coordinate their march.

On camera three, a group of 100 uniformed girls are steered by ten officers in a slow line near the Porta-Johns. There, three women drive them into shorter lines so they can use the toilets. Some of the girls use their orange caps as fans. (The woman watching the screens thinks how glad she is that she quit her job at the nursery selling mail-order plants and now works in an air-conditioned office, shielded from September's unbearable humidity.)

On camera four, 27 boys and 6 girls lined up in the center's parking lot. (When there are fewer than 100 individuals, the software reports an exact number of bodies and executes its facial recognition program.) Each one is carrying a bag. Five men accompany them as they get on a bus that reads DEPARTMENT OF CORRECTIONS. (The woman knows that these are the children who will be turned over to the custody of a family member while their asylum case is reviewed. As has happened before, she is happy for them and for a moment wishes them well, until she remembers the words of her president, who always repeats that the country must not become a sanctuary for intruders and criminals.)

On camera five, a large group of boys is corralled by seven adults to form a line along the yard outside the dormitories. They get them ready to go to the classroom hangar, where they will eat breakfast. Several are restless and don't stay in line. (She knows that they ran out of room in the cafeteria last week after the new group arrived.) Twelve boys who apparently tried to stay behind are forced back into formation.

On camera six, four hangars full of rows of cots where the children spend their nights. (Each time she looks at this screen, she imagines how hard it would be for her to sleep in a place like that.)

On camera seven, the small office assigned to visiting lawyers. (She hasn't figured out why, but she is relieved by the fact that it's almost always empty.)

On camera eight, the infirmary where two children wait alone on a single cot, their heads on either end. (She wonders again why they've cut the nurse's hours back to start at noon.)

On camera nine is the street that separates the center from the dense forest where the birds rest before continuing on their journey. The same thirteen old women who have been protesting for the past few months are planted out there on the sidewalk with their signs and their parasols.

FREE THE CHILDREN
NO HUMAN BEING IS ILLEGAL
END FAMILY SEPARATION NOW
KIDS DON'T BELONG IN DETENTION
CLOSE THIS CONCENTRATION CAMP!

(She likes that the camera is powerful enough to let her zoom in and read their signs. She notices that the one about the concentration camp is new, and that the women have added a large metal cage meant for an animal with a doll inside. She mutters the same curses as always and fantasizes about shouting something at the women as she drives past them on her way home. Don't they understand we're protecting their freedom? But she won't. She'll just glare at them and shake her head. In the staff meeting at the end of the week, she'll insist that the protesters interrupt their work and are bad for morale. That the police should really do something about them. Several of her colleagues will agree.)

On camera ten, an aerial view of the ground provided by the camera on the Customs and Border Protection radio tower. As always, the image is clouded by stains from the hundreds of vultures that sleep, vomit, urinate, and shit on the structure every day. A few of them can be seen on the metal rails, preening before the day's hunt.

On camera eleven, which was recently installed on the center's main security tower and affords a panoramic view of the entire perimeter, hundreds of birds cross above the fenced area that is beginning to fill with children. Their speed makes it hard to see them clearly. Since she started working there a few months earlier, she has never seen, on the cameras or with her own eyes, so many birds cleave the sky. (She wonders if some tragedy has befallen them. Or are they the sign of something to come? She will consult her pastor the following Sunday when she goes to church. He will recite a verse from the Bible: "Curse not the king, not even in thy thought; and curse not the rich even in the secret place of thy bedchamber; for the birds of the air shall spread the word, and those who have wings shall tell the matter." She will have a hard time seeing the connection between those words and the fleeting splotches that invaded her screens all week. A few days later, any interest she had in deciphering the flock will dissolve, just like the sandcastles her son makes at the beach melt away in the surf.)

The tanager is in the first wave to cross the prison's yards, but his wings beat too quickly for the woman to distinguish his entranced body among thousands of fast-moving creatures that interrupt her view of the choreography forced on these children from the south, who never imagined the north would be like this. Perhaps none of them notice the birds passing above the detention center, where their wandering lives have foundered. Not because they dislike winged creatures (many probably miss the birdsong of distant lands), but because exhaustion and the fear that someone is looking for them in vain are weakening their bodies, sucking the life from them. Where are they supposed to find the energy to look up at the open, blazing sky and remember all that is left of their journey?

For days, the tanager inadvertently accompanies the incarcerated children as he pecks away in the crowns of the rebellious trees, voraciously inhaling fruit, beetles, ants, and termites, amassing in his belly the wings, legs, and antennae of insects. A few times, he crosses the dry field where they march the children out once a day to be singed by the sun. After two weeks of feasting, his burgeoning chest and robust flank seem to tell him that his reprieve is over: it is time to continue on. To take advantage of the calm skies.

*

There is no way to know how he manages to cross the water without stopping. Or the substance of the impulse that hurls him through its vapors. What power has convinced him he can survive on the energy provided by insects and berries? What zeal in his wings tells him the enormous pit over which he flies for days and nights isn't the end of every world but rather a murmur announcing new flora? Where does the flame in his belly come from that assures him he can face any storm? These are days of furtive propulsion. Stellar and magnetic. Who knows—this we will never know—whether they are happy days.

He flies over the coast guard and other hulking ships that defend fantasies of dominating the waters. Who knows if he notices them from up high, as they flicker with an orphan glow that tries to distract him from the stars. He stops during the day with thousands more in a forest in the Cayman Islands, taking shelter from a storm that nearly broke while he was airborne. As the sun begins to set, he escapes the lurking peregrine falcon that swallows a hutia on the same branch of the copperwood where he is perched. Perhaps relief floods his chest when he alights on another tree. He shits. Before nightfall, he eats a dragonfly, three beetles, and numerous ants.

When he recovers his course across the open sea, he passes above a fugitive crocodile swimming north in search of an island. Neither one will see the other, of course, busy as they are scanning opposite horizons from air and water. No cosmic eye is needed to glean that at some point in the night, in the intimacy of tide and vapor, bird and reptile are connected nonetheless. The tanager, beating the air with anxious wings in search of solid ground where the highland forest awaits him. The crocodile, furiously beating the water with webbed feet in search of a shore far from the river where they tried to kill and skin him for handbags. They are bound together too by the cloudy waters where the crocodile stirred sediment and history, which flow into the same unfamiliar sea that the bird will cross on his way to respite on mountains that survive by mist from that river.

*

He reaches the rain forests of Darién after a long crossing through clouds that cloak rough seas; starving and thirsty, perhaps, but safe from further storms. Maybe he feels welcomed as he descends into the braided fronds, by all the rustling and buzzing and screeching and hissing and hooting and howling and clucking and cawing and squawking and dripping, by this commotion unknown to the stingier forests up north. Maybe he is excited by the impatient explosion of fruits that seem to have ripened for the sole purpose of receiving thousands of newcomers like him. Perhaps, in a place where everything scratches and invades, where everything is someone's snack or morsel, a tangle of fibers announces the possibility of shelter. Perhaps this viscous world populated by mud and moss, impregnated with sap and spore, where everything unfurls its power with noise and aroma, lets him know that there are only a few days left in his journey. The rain that rolls down the stems of that tribe of plants and fungi, where complicity is constantly sealed and undone, does not seem to worry him. Nor do the large drops that caress the back of his neck before lapping at tree trunks and muddying the mud, swelling the rivers, and rousing the frogs. He seems at home among the waters and mist that support the trees' journey from roots to sky.

On his second day of rest and feasting, the tanager escapes an attack by a praying mantis camouflaged on the branch of his usual mahogany, ready to devour the head of her prey. Who knows if the bird laments needing to abort his own hunt for a beetle that has laid its eggs nearby. Perhaps out of caution, he will not return to that tree. Or perhaps he has other reasons.

A few days before he sets out again, once he has provisioned his insides, he is startled by the turbine of a small aircraft that grazes the forest's dome. He might not perceive the rays of the sensor that two scientists from the Ancient Forest Observatory point at the canopy to measure the height of the tallest trees and report the carbon they store. The device certainly does not register the tanager as he perches on the branch of a cocobolo. Through a small window, the Emberá shaman who works as a guide for the scientists watches all the birds that take off as the airplane passes by and worries that the machine is upsetting the animals' mothers, the spirits of the water and the aquatic plants, all the creatures who live there and who are also the souls of his dead. He is unsettled by the thought that, from where he sits, he might be disturbing the king vulture that opens the gates to the world above. It is hard to see through such a small window and at that speed which birds are rising into the air, rattled by the aircraft. He imagines they are

kewarás

kumbarrás

sorrés

pipidís

widó-widós

jue-jues

and wonders if the winged motor that flusters the birds might disturb their flight and song to the point of breaking the bonds they sustain among the living things of all worlds. Whether the shock might prevent them from predicting the swell of rivers, the arrival of rains or iguanas, the impregnation of women. He thinks with horror that he is doing nothing to prevent this.

The Emberá shaman struggles to decipher the species of the tallest trees from above; trees whose whereabouts have been indicated by a satellite and that he has agreed to identify by name. He—who has since his childhood climbed so many trunks and clung to so many branches; who has spoken with the spirits of the rain forest and knows the curative souls of leaves, roots, and seeds; who sees visions of subterranean networks and branchings and has spent fifty years looking upward; who knows the different waters carried on the air by how they feel in his pores, who knows its foundations of muds and roots and the breath of its leaves when they are worried or glad—questions whether he knows his own forest. In their expeditions on foot, he has already identified wild cashews and shown them the oldest bongo and tonka trees he knows near their reserve. But now, far from the mud that supports them and the seeds that are their future, with the rumble of the aircraft silencing all animal chatter, inside a plastic enclosure that cancels out all the odors of the earth, at this altitude that is not his, the jaibaná loses his bearings.

The tanager is among the flurry of birds stirred into flight by the aircraft. When the pilot announces that they are approaching the border with Colombia and need to turn back, the shaman will again remember his tree in Salaquí, on the other side of this limit imposed by others, where he lived before the war forced him to flee into Panama with the rest of his town. He will interrupt the scientists' conversation about carbon, sensors, and satellites to tell them about the enormous wild cashew tree on the banks of the Jurachira that protected the reserve where he was born. In his uneven Spanish he will describe the broad, straight trunk bigger than any they have measured. He will liken its roots to walls and will say that he has never seen anyone like that being of vast, soft branches that flouts misfortune despite the centuries that pass. His grandparents of flesh and bone taught him that this leafy kin watched over his ancestors before the kampuniás came to colonize them. The wild cashew was the people's watchtower when the whites appeared with their horses and their thirst for war. He will explain how it has been the elders' duty ever since that tragic time to remind the others of this fact with their stories.

"Wise is that tree in Salaquí, that grandfather of mine."

One of the scientists will explain to him that of the fifty-two trees they registered that morning, several are probably between three and six centuries old. She will promise that when they process their data, they will make a model and an estimate of how many were alive before Columbus. That they will circulate the discovery in newspapers and magazines, and it will be good for the forest. She will be sorry they can't cross the border to measure his wild cashew. He will be sorry he can't run his hand over it fondly.

For a moment, the man will be grateful that someone has called the tree from which he is exiled his tree, though he knows it isn't true. He will imagine the joy of touching this relation again, of checking to see if it still weeps its aromatic sap, if grinding its leaves still releases the scent of sweet fruit, if it still changes each of its parts with the same zeal over the long passage of time. He will wonder, again, if it still accompanies anyone there or if it felt abandoned after the exodus. If someone came to try and cut it down or collect the cosmos held in its seeds. He will feel relieved that the scientists will not measure it, even if he doesn't say so.

The aircraft heads north over the dome of leaves and the threshold of petals that the tanager passed through not long before on his way south, in search of more food and less noise. The shaman senses him there, together with so many more, just like he does with his ancestors and kin, even if the bird remains unseen.

*

After a week of insects and fruits that plump his chest again and thicken his neck, the tanager takes off to cross the dense undulations of the rain forest. Who knows if the bird notices in the dark the scars in the earth where the miners razed the forest to forage for underground glimmers. And though he might not know it is gold they are looking for (or understand, in his life of vapors and vegetation, what this immortal metal means to people), perhaps he observes that the ground oozes neglect. He likely perceives the mercury burns, the bewilderment of roots and fungi, the age-old vigor of the trees fighting to recolonize the eroded dirt. There under the canopy, he might not be able to see the beams of flashlights held by people who have arrived from Africa, Venezuela, Cuba, and Haiti to cross the rain forest and continue into North America or hear the exhausted panting of the dogs who have traveled so far with some of them.

*

The journey is south and also ascent. Accompanying the rain forest as it scales the first buds of the cordillera. Rising along impatient layers from deep in the earth that have stretched to scrape the heavens for thousands of years. The tanager gathers misty air under his wings, tenses his tailfeathers, and aims the crown of his head toward the heights in order to gradually climb the thrusting surface of earth carpeted by thick forest and clouds that announce the end of the lowlands. As if his wings spread to welcome those tenacious folds. Perhaps he senses, as he feels the world wrinkle beneath him, that he is near the canopy where he will finally rest for a few months.

At dawn, assaulted by fatigue, he will need to find shelter among the root graveyards that interrupt the forest. Will he notice that the landscape was more green and lush on his last migration? Will sadness overtake him? None of the lonely trees clinging to life in the meadows of cattle or crops seem to appeal. He beats his wings until he finds some thick cover that has survived amid the carved-out cliffs at the foot of Dabeiba, a town peeking out from among mountains that observe one another. He enters an ancient forest that slopes toward a rushing stream. From high in the canopy, he can see the first rays of light announcing that strange hour when humans long for more night but the cosmos refuses.

Bursts of machine-gun fire echo nearby. Maybe he interprets the sound as thunder from a windless storm and concludes that he must first attend to his hunger and thirst, nourish his fading life force. When the helicopter passes, buffeting the canopy's humid calm, the tanager suspends his hunt to tighten his grip on a branch until the machine finally moves on. Despite the disarray of his feathers, perhaps he feels relief when he hears the clamor of the forest again, the cicadas and the crickets, though the echo of weapons continues on a neighboring mountain.

Interrupting his breakfast, a small aircraft soon arrives with its din and its drizzle of fine, white rain. Most of the poison falls on the crops but some also reaches the trees where the tanager rests, the ones that survived the last logging, in the form of a toxic dew that burns flesh and clouds eyes. A spray that leaves wings sticky and flecks berries, changing flavors and stinging the tongue. An acrid puddle staining iron that has long mingled gently with water. A cutting bitterness. Pain, maybe?

Everything begins to chitter again as the aircraft flies off. The bug-hungry bird makes his way to the riverbank and lands on a centenarian ceiba tree. Perhaps the water lapping at the rocks drowns out the voices of a little girl, her mother, and her dog, who have stopped nearby to wash off the poison. The mother steps out of the river and lets the water drip out of her clothes while she kicks at the stones in a rage.

"Now I know why I heard the striped owl last night."

"Why, Ma? What did it say?"

The girl lifts the reluctant dog and carries it into the water with her.

"They announce danger. No one taught you that? It's infallible. I thought it was your auntie's cancer getting worse. Should've known it was those army sonsabitches come to spray our crop."

The girl wonders what *infallible* means.

"But what if we wash the leaves, Ma?"

"The damage is done, love. The coca will be dead before sunset. And everything around is just as screwed, you'll see. That's how it is with those bastards the government sends. They come and destroy everything like it was nothing."

"Let's find a toucan, then."

The girl's grandfather told her once that drinking water out of anything a toucan took a sip from would bring good luck, and she has gotten in the habit lately of trying to soothe her mother whenever she gets angry over things that should make her sad.

"Listen to this one."

"I mean it. Aren't there toucans around here? If they live in these trees, then I'm sure they come down here to drink from the river. We can drink some of this water and I know it'll fix everything. Or at least make it a little better. What do you say?"

"Don't even think about drinking that water right now. They might be spraying upstream too, where all those crops are. Anyway, I haven't seen a toucan around here for a long time."

"Do the planes scare them off?"

The mother doesn't answer. Instead, she tells her daughter to go look for hummingbirds. She has taught her that seeing them in flight can improve your fate.

Upstream, the tanager splashes uneasily in a shallow pool formed by the river. Perhaps he feels lighter after washing off the resin caked on his feathers and the bitter smell of poison. Downstream, the girl walks along the rocks, scouring the trees until she tires of finding nothing but mosquitoes, butterflies, and wasps. When the din of the helicopters that she knows mean war finally fades into the distance, she hears so much chirping that she's certain one of those birds must be the kind that tells of good things to come.

Months later, after mother and daughter have padlocked their home, abandoned their shriveled crop, sold the cow and two chickens, and taken the dog with them to live with an aunt in Medellín, the girl will think every night about the forest where she played hide-and-seek with her cousins and the river she visited until the day of the poison. She will remember the sound of its rushing waters when she goes to the Parque de los Pies Descalzos with her mother to sell candy and cell phone minutes. The excitement of city kids splashing barefoot in the fountains will seem ridiculous to her. She will want to brag that she once lived next to a real river with toucans and hummingbirds, and that this park pales in comparison to the currents she knew back home. In the end, though, she will just glare at them from the corner.

At one point, she will encounter a real toucan in the wild animal sanctuary where her teachers at the foundation for displaced children will take her on a field trip. Before this unsettling vision, she will see other creatures that escaped catastrophe. She will feel relieved that the jaguar gnawing on a bone seems happy not to be the pet of a drug lord anymore, though his new landscape is also fenced in. And that the sloth seems to be at peace, even though the truck that ran him over left him with only three paws. That the seven morrocoy turtles can swim to their hearts' content in the sanctuary's channels after years of living in jars and crates. That the iguana can deftly climb an orange tree instead of spending her days trying to ignore the rocks thrown at her through the bars of her cage in a hotel in Capurganá. That the capuchin monkeys, especially the one whose hand had been mutilated, are swinging from branches instead of being chained to the arms of the men who tried to sell them along the road to Urabá. That the macaw with the shattered beak no longer needs to face his tormentor or dream of breaking free from the cord that bound him for so long to a metal bar. That the orange-winged parrots can take solace in the trees growing under nets as they wait to be returned to the Amazon after surviving weeks of darkness inside boxes that slammed against one another in trucks and propeller planes; that they escaped the fate of being sent to Europe in the cargo hold of a ship loaded with sugar.

Only at the end, when the girl is searching for somewhere to sit and cry, will she see her perched on the branch of a wild cashew tree, her huge beak bursting shameless from her yellow face. A sword that seems like pure artifice, as if the bird's body existed only to support that riot of color. In awe, the girl will press herself against the bars of the cage to watch her shred a papaya while flouting any notion of camouflage. She will admire the red, orange, and blue spots that interrupt the green of her beak, as if new colors were about to be born there, colors she'd never seen before. She will wonder if someone painted the fine lines that cross it and whether the bird drinks blood every day to keep its tip that shade of crimson. She will think of that beak as shears to cut even the strongest flower:

a magical box, a queenly blade. She will envy that bright case, which protects a long tongue able to taste whatever it desires, something she cannot do.

She will listen, rapt, as the guide explains that this female toucan, now named Guapa, was found early that year in the parking lot of a Medellín shopping mall. She will ask when they are going to release her and will be sad to learn that the bird wouldn't survive in the forest after living in the city for so long.

"Could somebody adopt her?"

The guide will laugh. Then the girl will search desperately for the dish where the bird dips her colors but will not find it. She will feel an intense desire to drink the water that has touched that beak and a fierce hunger to tear it off and scratch her skin with it, to caress the world with it, mixing elements. She will think that when she is older, she will get a job rescuing stolen animals, saving wild animals from the people who snatched them from the forests to sell them. That night, she will tell her mother that she wants to be a police officer who specializes in protecting living creatures, not the kind that destroys crops. What she will not reveal (afraid that her mother will dash her hopes) is that she wants to do this work so she can one day rescue a toucan from wrongful captivity and drink the miraculous water transformed by its beak. To bring back their good luck.

Upstream, between clasped branches and fruits ripe to the point of bursting, the tanager moves farther and farther from the woman and her daughter. Once he is sated, he twists and fans his wings to dig around in his feathers, removing the parasites that have settled there along the way. The girl and her mother wait all afternoon in the drizzle beside the foamy riverbank, bored of slapping away mosquitoes, until the sound of helicopters is finally replaced by the hooting of owls. Only then do they set out with the dog for their poisoned home. As if all that thundering had broken his momentum, the tanager spends another day brushing his small body against the rebellious foliage of that forest where everything pulses and bears witness. Perhaps he is confused by the war, which still echoes nearby. By its strong wind, which doesn't smell like the leaves or flutter them gently from below. Its strange smoke. Its intermittent din. Its white liquid.

*

It is hard work, rising and falling with mountains that ascend ever higher. Who knows where he finds the strength to climb the spine of lands that fold, sink, arch, and gather. To fly over vast rivers that glint like mirrors in distant valleys. To eye streams that defy the peaks' upward surge. To cross patches of cloud that gravitate toward the slopes and tangle in branches, sacrificing themselves. To breathe air that grows lighter and makes his heart fight harder than it should.

Luckily, the tanager evades the great glare of Medellín, which glitters far off to one side. Other birds will not be so fortunate. As almost always happens in Octobers and Aprils, he is doused by the bellicose clouds of the cordillera; there is no way to know if he feels any fear at the lightning bursts he sees on nearby mountains. The Magdalena River makes its presence known in the small hours, once the bird has left the steepest peaks of his sojourn behind. Perhaps he notices, from way up there, the valley's peaceful abundance. Maybe he is unaware that the water's currents, resigned to dissolving life into sediment, are exhausted from dragging mud and bone. He drives the crown of his head downward to tame the air that thickens with his descent. It could be because the river is flanked by fields and marsh that, despite the exhaustion of crossing two mountain ranges, the bird postpones his landing until he reaches the tree-lined hills that mark the end of the valley and the beginning of new peaks.

The tanager spends two days resting in a forest that is desperately trying to replenish the vast dwelling that crops and cattle stole years ago; he devours the bulging fruits of guamas, aguacatillo and guava trees, and coffee plants. Does he know which other birds reached those branches around the same time? Does he sense their nomadic strength? See them as his equals?

When he sets out again, he encounters thousands of them kneading the night sky. The geolocator that sends a signal to the International Space Station from the back of a gray-cheeked thrush has no way of conveying the fact that a scarlet tanager has joined the enormous flock at those coordinates and for a while beat its wings beside the little brown bird.

Only a Little While Here

*

An age-old command seems to propel him upward into the colder daybreaks of this new cordillera, where Andean blueberries and the fruits of the arrayán grow. With great effort, he unfurls his lightness to graze the peaks of ever-taller mountains and jumbles skies that had once been guarded by condors in the days before most of them died. He flies over rocky cliffs and spiny frailejón. Will his movement slow on those summits smattered with low-lying shrubs, the way hikers slow their pace in the thin air at those heights? Horizon-keen, he races past clouds born of the river that float slowly upward, plump with their own gravity and their desire for verticality. Bird and vapor penetrate one another as they rise to later descend. Needles of water pierce his wings, but he flies on, unfazed, ignoring the drops that soak his beak and eyes.

    When the tanager finally reaches the highlands, the luminous splotch of Bogotá appears, discoloring the sky in the distance, confusing the night, and calling him off course. Beneath him, the city's westernmost streets begin to appear, empty only at that hour, as well as the airport with its airplane parasites and the warehouses of the industrial zone. Light shines off the water of a marsh, but he probably cannot see the pack of wild dogs resting beneath the alcaparro trees and the chusque. The downpour intensifies and overflows the sewers of a city that has always disregarded its waters. He flies east over the uneven heaps of rooftops and tanks, of antennae pretending to be mushrooms, until he finds trees grouped in a park. A veteran guayacan invites him to wait out the storm among its branches. He grabs hold and weathers the thunderclaps that lighten his attempted sleep. Perhaps he feels cold, now that he is so much bonier, and wonders how he can fill that void. Maybe he doesn't notice two stray dogs asleep under a concrete bench.

When the downpour becomes a drizzle and the light begins its struggle to wash white through heavy clouds, the tanager will set out in search of leafier branches. He seems to heed the call of the slopes that rise nearby. Perhaps the screeching of horns and brakes from the city's early stirrings grates on his nerves; he might know them to be the hollow imitations of an animal in distress. Maybe his inner reaches burn with the heavy, combustion-rank air.

But before he can seek asylum on the imposing mountain there is the mirror. A bank with sparkling windows that counterfeit the sky. The impact casts the bird into an opacity unlike the one he knows from sleep. No cleaning woman or manager working early to approve a loan bears witness as the bird slams its head against the thick pane of glass. The unrelenting habit of his wings might be the only thing that keeps him aloft after the blow, the only thing that prevents him from shattering against the pavement.

Perhaps in his stupefaction the walls and windows of the buildings around him seem to wobble and the world becomes a blur in which he cannot trust any tree. Who knows how the pain courses through him, or what fire scalds his disjointed neck. Whether the bruise on his crown or the mistreated joints between his wings howl at him. Perhaps he is tormented in the fibers of his back that house the strength to send him skyward.

Dazed, he descends to the third-floor balcony of a small building. The woman stepping out to hang a towel forgets the malaise pricking her coccyx when she encounters the bewildered bird on its granite surface. Seeing him so still, she wonders what happened to the alert gaze and balletic neck that any other bird would boast. Why does he show no sign of leaving? As if embalmed in the display case of some museum, the tanager ignores the water and grains of rice the woman leaves on the ground for him. Maybe he is terrified by the enormous body approaching him, as skittish and quick as he tends to be, though perhaps his fear remains bottled up inside him.

"What's wrong, little bird?"

For the first time, a human finger strokes his back and ruffles the red feathers hidden by his yellow coat. Could he still be too stunned to register the imposition? The woman feels the bird's racing heartbeat and chides herself for getting so close. She wants to apologize and suspects that she has violated an age-old law stating that free birds must not settle in any human eye. That no one should force them to be anything but ephemeral.

She wonders why the bird landed on her balcony, between the broom and the clotheslines, and not in the rubber tree next door, in the hundred-year-old Chinese ash down the street, or among the eucalyptus that tower nearby. She wants to believe that he chose her for her special connection with birds. Once, when she was a child, she was walking through a pasture on the finca where she grew up and noticed a flock of swallows swirling above her; when a little piece of shit fell from the sky right into her palm, she felt like she had been chosen by them. At an age when everything seemed a bit off, she decided that the bird's excrement resting on the midline of her hand (the line corresponding to her head, said the cook, an expert in palmistry) was indisputably a good omen and an offering. That was the same finca where she had helped swallows and hummingbirds with sugar water and care after they crashed their enthusiasm into the windows. She would cradle their stunned little bodies in her hands until the shock of the impact wore off, congratulating the survivors when they flew away, and burying the ones who died. But now, under the weight of years that turn many of us inward, she has a hard time imagining that the anguish of this little bird, cloistered in its paralysis, might be the result of a collision between a window and his relentless dedication to pilgrimage.

She likes the thought that the bird chose to land at her feet because he can sense how devoted she is to animals, how distraught she becomes whenever she considers the abuse they suffer, which is almost every day. The frustration that drives her to leave bones on street corners for stray dogs some nights, organize fundraisers for humane societies, and protest in front of the Plaza de Toros whenever there is a bullfight. The sense of urgency with which she recently rescued a dog from a highway rest stop after it was run over and then found it a home, convinced an aunt who lives in the countryside to take in one of the horses that had been forced to pull a cart along city streets, and tried to prevent her grandfather from fumigating the corn because it poisoned the bees. Her indignation at friends who refused her attempts to convert them to veganism.

Later, she chides herself for assuming that this unfamiliar bird is begging for her help and remembers all the intrepid creatures who have escaped their cages. She wonders if the bird on her balcony is out of sorts because it traded its captivity inside an apartment for the smoldering din of Bogotá. A few years prior, while she was studying in Boston, signs announcing lost pets posted around the neighborhood where she lived informed her of a mutiny of captive birds. The first was for a green parakeet with pink and black feathers on its throat; in the photo, a handsome specimen named Bandi perched elegantly on a finger.

In the months that followed, perhaps because her eye was already trained toward all those signs posted in the street, she noticed more announcements of desertions: a cockatoo, another parakeet, a parrot (with the unforgettable name of Lollipop), a one-footed pigeon (she couldn't imagine how it escaped), a canary. Always an owner declaring the bird's absence, begging neighbors to come to their aid and resolve their recent abandonment, to ease their newly imposed orphanhood. Always the large reward promised to any reader willing to turn their eyes skyward and locate the strange bird chirping among the leaves while all other winged creatures fled the cold buffeting those northern coordinates. As if those people failed to comprehend that the fugitive birds wanted to desert and to forget fingers, cages, the smell of frying meat, televisions, and tables; that they wanted to dust off their atrophied wings and finally understand trees. Did their mutiny point to something larger, something about the miserable state of the world? In the dark months she spent studying, she had been happy for those unruly birds. She would send them telepathic messages of strength and encouragement to persevere in their exodus, knowing they couldn't hear her.

A biologist friend told her back then about scientific studies performed on migratory birds in captivity. About how—early in autumn or spring, when their kind would begin to move—the caged birds would become frenetic, jumping around and flapping their wings in desperation, slamming against the bars, suffering from insomnia. Experts had been studying this distress for decades, observing and measuring their torture, in order to prove the theory that birds perceive the minutiae of interplanetary choreographies and calibrate their inner clocks to cosmic time when making their journeys. Science disemboweling the mystery of the nomad in order to name it.

Zugunruhe

From the German *Zug*, movement or migration, and *Unruhe*, restlessness or disquiet. It was when she went looking for more information on birds in captivity that she stumbled across the word a German ornithologist used in 1707 to describe their symptoms. The perturbation of a few peripatetic birds for whom stillness is the only exile. A word to mask the infamy of the culprits, to try and name a conviction beyond what we humans call free will. She had forgotten the term when she came back from the United States; only now, with the tanager paralyzed before her, does it return to her mind.

She doesn't care if she's late to work. She finds hundreds of photographs of scarlet tanagers online—males with red feathers that turn ochre according to the season, yellow females—on branches spread over most of the continent. Their scientific name, common names, and the regions inhabited by the species. Also a map that connects with colorful arrows the northeast, where they mate and incubate their eggs, the tropical zones they pass through during migration, and the Andean mountains, where they avoid what in their northern groves we call winter. The list of details seems obscene in the face of the tenuous vitality of the bird that does not appear to have found its power out on the balcony. She goes out to find him still there, petrified. Could he have landed there to die? She learns that a male was tagged in Pennsylvania in 1990 and found in Texas in 2001. All that distance, at least twenty-four times. It pains her not to know how many trips this one has made.

She is moved to think that this figure of continental sojourn, this proof of sovereign nomadism, rests so close to her.

She knows it is an overstatement, but she likes to think that the tanager did not land on her balcony by coincidence: they have these crossings in common, even if she was born in the south and he in the north, even if the winged creature's journeys consist of different currents and many more stops. She would like to conclude that the two are bound together by these comings and goings and by their shared love of an intense sun that doesn't exist in the winter. That these things attune one to the other and make them somehow equal.

She watches the tanager for a while longer from the balcony doorway until she can only conclude that the bird ignoring her is not pleading for help or recognition. She thinks she understands his demand for solitude and senses that he is exhausted by sorrows she could never fathom. Before leaving him, she takes a picture.

In the years that follow, this image of the bird against the cracked granite will be a talisman that cheers and unsettles her, just like the little cards of Our Lady of Sorrows and martyred saints that believers keep in their wallets. The tanager will wink at her as the background of her laptop until the computer is stolen one day and she loses all the files she didn't back up, after which she will never see it again.

Only a Little While Here

For a long time, the woman will ask herself why that bird revealed himself to her on the empty balcony of a building where she would live until layoffs began at the National Archive a few months later. When she returns to the United States with an onerous loan to secure another degree, she will obsess over the tanager again. She will speculate about the journeys he might have made since then, hoping he is still alive, and will be excited to think that just as their paths crossed in the south, perhaps the bird has flown over her while returning to summer in some forest in the same northeast where she is trying to build a new life. So she will search for scarlet tanagers in the groves of Pennsylvania every weekend each spring, when bare trunks begin to quiver with landings and song. She will last several months, paying off a set of fancy binoculars and rubbing her pollen-dusted eyes until she wishes she could just scratch them out. She will try to learn the tanager's call from recordings she finds online, even though she has a hard time remembering it. She will check, daily, the radar maps tracking aerial migrations and the website where sightings reported in real time appear on a map of the continent as little red flags. It will pain her not to be able to see the millions of migrating birds take over the night skies in April and September, though she searches for them from the little balcony of her rented apartment. Despite her terrible memory, she will make an effort to identify more species. She will try not to be disappointed when she sees sedentary birds, the ones who prefer to stay and face the horrifying cold; in the winter, when everything around her seems to have died, she will begin to admire them. In May, when she recognizes one that has come from the south, she will shout a greeting that will echo through the forest, not caring if nearby hikers shoot her strange looks.

In seven years of searching she will never see a scarlet tanager, though she often thinks she can hear them up high in the oaks, and other people with binoculars she encounters on the trails confirm their arrival. Until one day in June; walking through a forest near Philadelphia filled with voracious ticks, she recognizes a

teeet teeeet teeeyooeet teeet

and glimpses a haughty male up at the top of a new-leafed cedar, a flash of red and song.

She will try to film him with her cell phone, but the video will only capture the swaying foliage and the ruckus of many birds. She will tell her friends about the sighting but feel disappointed when none shares her sense of wonder.

Around that time, a woman she dates for only a little while, who speaks only English and has not traveled much, will press her to name the reasons behind her obsession, which had before nested wordlessly in the folds of her viscera, like a mystery. It will be when the woman no longer has any choice but to recognize that she has been settling into Philadelphia and that the reciprocal coming and going between two lands isn't a simple thing. She will have married a friend for the green card that exempts her from spending her days begging for temporary visas. She will have gotten a job at a foundation dedicated to prison reform that will pay her just enough to live on and to make a monthly donation to a sanctuary for abused animals in Cartagena. She will have adopted a cat from the shelter where she volunteers and will reluctantly have begun to learn the names of the gringo trees she tried so long to ignore, names she will often forget when their branches are bare.

In an English that always makes her feel uncertain and imprecise, she will explain to her lover that migratory birds fascinate her because, in their undulations that blur the line between heaven and earth, they turn every niche in the world into a brief home, even as their wings insist that nothing is ever inhabited on a permanent basis. Guests of the sky, where there is no shelter, they ignore the nefarious borders invented by humans and scorn their rage at foreigners. No one can shout Go back to your fucking country! at them to hurt their feelings (like they will scream at her one day). Though the bird may be halted in its journey by drought or cold, by a hungry predator or countless man-made obstacles, it is not eaten away by longing. It defiles every boundary and is always immersed in the mixture, not off to the side or in the margins, but right there in the weave of the world, which includes skies, where residence is irrelevant.

She doesn't want to admit it, but the woman obsessed with tanagers will finally understand that she envies these itinerant birds; she is jealous of their capacity to inhabit ambiguity without torment, to defy with their lightness the hardships that plague her. Of how they serenely accept the cosmic mandate constantly inviting them to return (at least, she believes they do). She, on the other hand—who has spent a decade of (increasingly sporadic) travels back and forth between the north and south of the continent, between the gringo forests with their signposted trails, low hills, and traffic noises where no one says hello, and the winding foggy paths of the Andes that she visits only briefly now—feels that back-and-forth braid through her body as awe and unease. Every arrival in the north after time in the south torments her with specters that activate her nostalgia, even if she finds it trite and always tries to shake it off like dust. Every apartment she inhabits will stir in her the overwhelming promise of rootedness, followed by the threat of captivity. The change of pillow, of clouds, of north, of water, will pain her, but this will not stop her. She will feel joy and then annoyance when, after a trip to Colombia, she finds seeds of highlands grass (her grandmother always called them "amores") clinging to her clothes despite airplanes and washing machines. Try as she might, she will not be able to ignore the vegetal magnetism, the visceral pull of the air and the bark of mountains she climbed as a child, though she spends most of the year far from them. In the darkest, barest days of winter, when the migratory birds have finished their lucid fugue, she will feel the tug of the distant cordillera like a branch striking between her vertebrae. She will know there is no healing this wound that refuses to clot. And even though she thinks about living in Bogotá again, and sometimes even promises herself that she will, she will make no real effort to return.

As she will clarify for this fleeting girlfriend, what fascinates her is that migratory birds unhesitatingly trust their lives to fronds and the flow of currents, even when the branches beneath them shake. When they rest along their way, their only roots belong to the tree under their feet. Their journey is not an exodus but rather the celebration of perpetual transition. Visitors by nature, they courageously embody their solitude, though sometimes they raise young or beat their wings as a flock. They seek neither to belong nor to escape, whereas people like her, or maybe people in general, get stuck in those mournful commonplaces.

She will finally be able to articulate that she is amazed by the birds' pilgrimage to the forest, their reverence for thriving bud and living leaf that drives them from the wintry cold she so detests. The loyal conversation they maintain with sun and tree. Their constant journey toward the spirit of vegetation, toward the most ebullient time of the leaf.

She will feel insulted when the other says that birds actually migrate in order to stay at home, since they're looking for familiar conditions in the two places, and will ask how dare she compare one forest with the other, especially without ever having traveled there; she will shut this lover up by telling her that she sounds like a typical gringo.

She will push further, adding that a migratory bird would be the first to realize that trees in the tropics don't suffer months of stoic dormancy and that their sap runs at a different pace. That foliage tangles differently there.

Fully grasping the roots of her adoration and envy, the woman will understand that although she and the bird are crossed by many of the same northern and equatorial fronds, they will never be equals. (She will not find a match in that lover, either. She will hate her dream of buying a house in the suburbs. Her fear of insects and her love of winter. That she says "we" when talking about the government. She will resent how awkwardly she climbs rocky trails and how she trips over every root. Her mistrust of the forest. They will leave each other not long after the one who venerates birds stops asking the one who couldn't care less about them to join her searches among the trees.)

The tanager escapes his trance on the balcony of northern Bogotá just a few minutes before the woman peeks out to check on him again. The grains of rice remain untouched, like the water in the platter (years later, the woman will conclude that she should have left him a piece of fruit split open). Perhaps it was his fierce nomadic mandate that stirred him from his stupor, she thinks. A kind of *Zugunruhe*. Saddened that the tanager left no trace of his presence, she crouches to look for bird shit on the granite but finds none.

※

No human could know how the tanager manages to ignore the burn of his bruises, regain his bearings, and take off in search of a denser forest. He flies through the drizzle above the city buildings until he reaches the drenched mountains. He ascends to a peak where Bogotá becomes a hoarse and irritable secret. How does hunger roar in him? Does he feel pain erupt inside? The bird finds no insects on the wet eucalyptus and pine branches. There are no berries, either. Perhaps he feels his heartbeat more forcefully since the flesh that once cushioned his organs has melted away.

※

Ignoring, perhaps, the fire that throbs in his tendons and bones, that night the tanager rises desperate to complete this final stretch. He skirts mountains that halt the city and crosses a plateau where lights are scarce. He ascends rocky bluffs and tall summits, then flies over a lake that is drying out, despite its glimmer. Someone unfamiliar with his voyage might confuse his exhaustion with a loss of direction.

There is no way to know how the tanager recognizes his usual mountain among all the cloud-logged crests. What flight nerve tells him he has reached the dwelling that welcomed him before, that he has arrived at the end of the road? He crosses the fog to descend into the forest of his past. Who knows if disappointment or doubt creeps in when he finds in its place a tiered pasture that announces the extermination of romerones, oaks, gaques, encenillos, higuerón and arrayán trees, suscas, cedars, and black pines. Now, eleven cows desirous of grass graze among the corpses of huge trunks. The tanager has no way of knowing what has happened to the trees that years earlier held him and so many beetles and spiders, porcupines, butterflies, and moths. How the mineral intelligence of millions of roots hungrily seeking the center of the earth was abruptly extinguished. Can he sense the sorrow emanating from what was razed? Maybe the question of this absence arises in him, somehow.

Perhaps the tanager recognizes the surviving oak in the middle of the pasture when he lands there as if searching for somewhere to recover from the confusion. Maybe he knows that he perched there before and feels the welcome of the living tree still embraced by bromeliads, fungi, and ferns. Who knows if he hears a vaporous bewilderment rise from its leaves or if he senses its cries over the absence of its tribe, over bonds cleaved by a chain saw. Maybe he can understand, resting on the muscles of the trunk, the consternation of roots that search for other living tentacles and find none. The still-intact desire to interweave with others. The rebellious drive of age-old branches that continue tossing out new seeds and birthing enthusiastic offspring, though the cows relentlessly chew them up. The bird's leathery toes squeeze the branch cushioned by lichens and moss and are drenched. Who knows if these creatures are joined in their hope that somewhere in that air and in those fibers is a surviving nerve that might restore the community.

On the highest branch of this gigantic tree, the tanager waits for dawn to fully break so he can peer over the highlands and hills expanding before him, where the fog is beginning to dissolve. Then he seems to find the last bubble of brio in his chest and takes to the air again. He flies over a flowering potato crop being fumigated by several men, and over more tilled lands, more pastures with cows, and over a foot trail with glistening puddles, until he reaches a new hill where trees hundreds of years old huddle close together, satisfied, in the unending labor of weaving the skin of the slope.

A thick grove of oaks rises, generous, behind a small house. A few dogs bark. The carriquí jays intone their clamor. He must be relieved. Isn't he? Perhaps something like happiness or solace stirs within him. Maybe he knows that by landing in that cloud forest after all those detours, from the moment he entrusts himself to those crooked fronds and immerses himself in the tumult, nothing will be foreign to him. At least for a while, until the cosmos orders him to return.

III

To Walk These Lands

To walk these lands = quycas isyne
In the land = hichatana, l, hischy cuspquana

—Anonymous,
Dictionary and Grammar of the Chibcha Language,
early seventeenth century

Behold this compost! behold it well!
[...]
Now I am terrified at the Earth, it is that calm and patient,
It grows such sweet things out of such corruptions,
It turns harmless and stainless on its axis, with such endless successions of diseas'd corpses,
It distills such exquisite winds out of such infused fetor,
It renews with such unwitting looks its prodigal, annual, sumptuous crops,
It gives such divine materials to men, and accepts such leavings from them at last.

—Walt Whitman, "This Compost"

Tankayllu is the name of the inoffensive humming insect that flies through the fields sipping nectar from the flowers. The *tankayllu* appears in April, but may be seen in irrigated fields during other months of the year. Its wings whir at a mad pace to lift its heavy body with its ponderous abdomen. [. . .] Children hunt it to sip the honey with which the false stinger is anointed. [. . .] because its wings make such a loud noise, much too strong for such a tiny figure, the Indians believe that the *tankayllu* has something more inside its body than just its own life. Why does it have honey on the end of its abdomen? Why do its weak little wings fan the air until they stir it up and make it change direction? How is it that whoever sees the *tankayllu* go by feels a gust of air on his face? It cannot possibly get so much vitality from such a tiny body. It fans the air, buzzing like a big creature; its velvety body disappears, rising straight upward into the light. No, it is not an evil being; children who taste its honey feel for the rest of their lives the brush of its comforting warmth on their hearts, protecting them from hatred and melancholy.

—José María Arguedas,
Deep Rivers, tr. Frances Horning Barraclough

She has survived exile before. The first time was the zeal of a hoe they used to break up the earth of her home at the base of an elderberry tree to plant chard in a new vegetable garden. Back then, she was young and spongy. Just one month earlier, she had burst the unctuous membrane of the egg that housed her and emerged to drag her larval serenity through dust and minerals. The day when everything around her began to shake and the lumps that embraced her loosened their grip and the tool tossed her through the air, she was spared from being sliced in two by the metal edge. From having the viscous juices of decomposed leaves that kept her plump leak through a tear in her side, as happened to a few of her siblings. When she fell back to earth, the fat rolls of her larval body cushioned her and the hard shell still armoring her head protected her from the impact. She managed to gather the wormly length she would bear patiently for another month as her thorax and wings matured, defenseless, inside. Then she turned herself facedown and hauled the dense accordion of herself through the mud until she was again inside the blackness of mycorrhizae and stone, between which more clouds than usual were beginning to filter, thanks to their new disarray.

Someone might say that now, two months after hoe stirred earth, as she prepares to leave her pupal self behind, her nomadic life is just beginning. Or else it is the beginning of her string of mistakes, which for many is the same thing as leaving. She eagerly tears at the hide of that underground home that held her for a time while she was building herself better. She sheds her own borders (perhaps without nostalgia) and says goodbye to the slippery, squishy life of a white larva to announce that she is a beetle shielded by brown armor. That she will continue tilling the earth with her bulk, but differently now. (Who hasn't announced the same thing on occasion?) She stretches her legs, getting them ready to carry this solid, convex new body, and heads out to sidestep roots, rub herself against dust, stoically battle rocks and clumps, face the humid night air. She has not eaten any leaves since she was a larva and is probably assailed by hunger. Perhaps after three weeks asleep underground her jaw is a bit stiff; she might need to loosen it in order to devour foliage again, now better than before.

Unfurling her wings for the first time and activating them under the weight of her armature seems to pose a challenge. Debuting them in a brief, awkward first flight, like a firework that shoots crooked after being in storage too long. Perhaps she is unmoved by her new cellophane buzzing and her stepless journey, accepting them as an inclination she has always carried. Maybe she means to land in the garden next to the house, right beside the chewed-up plants struggling to grow despite the downpours and the invasion of beetles like her in

November. She advances slowly, dodging stems and lumps in the ground, suffering the sway of her thorax, which threatens always to flip her over. Some would say she is all effort and ineptitude, but now that she has shed her larval length and is able to fan the air, she likely feels more agile than ever. She wobbles as she advances leg by leg through the uneven mud, which for a small insect like her must seem like crossing a mountain range. She struggles to maintain her balance on each clump of dirt that ambushes her and slowly climbs a pile of dog shit. As if by accident, her claws scratch the eggs flies have laid there.

She joins the slender-legged shuffle of more experienced beetles as they mate, eat, land, and take off. She must sense the aromas they emit into the fog to let one another know they're there, scratching away at the earth, ready to mount and rub and fertilize eggs, if the rain allows. On her way through the freshly planted ferns, the june bug passes close by a spider carrying dozens of eggs on her back. She probably has no interest in the lightness the other flaunts. The armored one skirts stems, mushrooms, and sleeping crickets before sinking her mandibles into the fallen leaf of a hydrangea. She devours her first bite as a beetle. Perhaps the bitter juices and powdery mildew staining the leaf fill her with insectile joy the likes of which we could never imagine. Though perhaps she should be concerned, she seems not to notice the song of the potoo, who with the arrival of darkness has given up imitating the stillness of bark and has finally opened its huge yellow bird-of-prey eyes to track the insects in the vegetable garden and swallow whatever crunchy thorax presents itself to him. Who knows if the june bug hears the clamor of the frogs as they syncopate the night's teeming from one of the garden's water sources. She plots to slice and suck more mouthfuls of fresh leaf from another hydrangea with the sharp edges of her front arsenal. Perhaps she needs to sate herself after her long entombment. She moves so slowly that she appears to be asleep.

When she sets out again, she slips into a puddle beside a bed of calla lilies left by the afternoon's downpour. For a moment, she floats in the mud. What anguish must be swirling beneath her armature as she kicks frantically in the black water? She manages to grab hold of a stick, climbs to the edge, and remains there for a while, as if waiting for the drops on the fine threads that coat the bottom of her abdomen to dry. A pause that must feel to her like a lifetime.

Leaving the garden, she takes off in eager flight toward the powerful lantern hanging in the courtyard of the house, around which dozens of moths dance, moon-confused. Despite the puddle water, her wings seem more elastic and buzz with greater force. She hurls herself toward the light with such zeal that she bumps against the bulb and falls to the ground. This is the first time she has suffered the catastrophe of flailing on her back, forced against her will to face the sky. Who knows if she is bothered when her antennae graze the tiles as she struggles to right herself. Maybe she notices the other beetles engaged in a similar riot of mute, despairing kicks. For an hour, she battles the armature that is there to save her from impacts but now disrupts her north. With a bobbing of trochanter and femur, with a shake of tibia and tarsal, her claws strum the tiny drops of cloud beginning to settle on the mountain. She probably detects the anguished vapors that the others emit as they struggle to see the ground again, as their strength wanes, as they doze from the strain, as they resign themselves to forever longing for the earth. Who knows if, in this upside-down world that currently weighs on her, the june bug can see the nearby corpse of another beetle, accidentally disemboweled by the home's owner hours before, the white fat peeking out from her rear end like the materialization of her dying breath. Is she moved by the death of those like her? Perhaps she, relegated until so recently to the muddy depths, is unaware that birds and mice tend to visit this cemetery of exhausted creatures to break their fasts. But she doesn't seem like the kind to drag every potential predator around with her in a state of paranoia, or to always be ready to make an escape. She is not as ephemeral as the fly or as light as the cricket, nor is she as swift as the moth. It is as if she didn't care that the world can be pure danger.

A dog makes his way to the garden to sniff the nocturnal animals he never knew in Bogotá. Perhaps he's looking for opossums, which give off an oily musk that seems to drive him wild. His tail whips against the stalks of flowers planted by the woman who recently moved there with him. He sticks his muzzle into the hole he dug that morning when he caught the scent of mice, but nothing there seems to excite him anymore. He inhales the vapor filtering through the wax laurel that the last opossum he chased climbed into days ago, but he finds no recent traces. Fragrances of flesh and fur and spines and rot reach him from a distance to engorge his nose. But everything is dark and damp, and after a brief sampling the dog appears to conclude that it isn't the moment for pursuing other muzzles. He lets out an aimless bark, and his urine splatters on two beetles and a cricket. On the way to his bed (he sleeps outside ever since leaving the city), he comes across the june bugs languishing on the patio. He grew out of puppyhood a little while ago, but sometimes he still feels that frantic drive to play with any living thing that moves. He approaches the exhausted beetle, which has stopped her furious kicking to right herself, and nudges her with the tips of his claws, containing his strength so as not to squash her altogether, as if coaxing her into staying alive. He pushes her a little with his nose and then with his paw, urging her to escape so he can catch her again, like he does with the mice he recently learned to hunt among fallen oak leaves. As if stirred from her resignation, she wraps her legs around the dog's fur and clings to one of his toes. Startled by this plea for help, he shakes his paw and slams its pads against the ground until he sends her tumbling across the paving stones. She bounces a few times and then rights herself. Did the impact dislocate something? Does she feel relieved to be facing the ground again? The dog runs toward the woman who is calling him to lie down and forgets about the beetle forever.

Only a Little While Here

The june bug traverses the flagstones lit through the glass door. The beetles take advantage of the fact that the construction workers who finished the house just a few months earlier miscalculated and left too much space between the doors and the ground, failing to consider insects or the rainy season. She crosses the threshold and enters the house, captivated by the ethereal hoax that distracts her from mating and laying eggs. The glow of the light bulbs must be irresistible for her because she interrupts her climb and descent of the fibers of the first carpet she encounters to take off in the direction of a lamp. This time she whirs over without incident and lands on a nearby curtain.

Who knows if she notices the white moth also clinging to the fabric. A warmer light soon breaks her addiction to that first flash; she readies her wings and flies toward the fixture hanging in the middle of the dining room. She circles around it several times, but its blaze is clearly inhospitable, and she can't figure out where to rest her body to fuse with the filaments. Like a disoriented parachuter, she descends in circles to the table. Clothes left there by the home's owner soften her landing. The hooks on her legs catch on the threads of a sock. She tries to take flight, but the fibers detain her. It takes her a long time, tugging on each branch of her body, to disentangle herself.

She flies toward the powerful light in the kitchen, its glare a siren song calling her to fatally dash her armature against it. The impact knocks her onto the counter among all the food laid out there, but this time she is lucky enough to land upright. In her stillness, she seems to grope for which way to go next. Perhaps she is drawn to the smell of the nearby chard, which came from the garden just like she did. She advances laboriously across the slippery granite toward the vegetable, ignoring a few beetles on their backs, already dead, until she reaches the fibrous red stalk. Is she relieved to recognize the verdure she deserves? She scales its surface to the wrinkled peace of a leaf that seems to fold her into an embrace. She must be exhausted after so much fluttering. She bites, sucks, guzzles, swallows, destroys its fibers at her leisure. Shits. Maybe she is beset by a need to copulate, by the desire of the eggs inside her for their own plot of land.

How will she realize they sealed off the sky? Perhaps she senses a different air inside the plastic bag where she and the chard have been imprisoned. The cold of the refrigerator probably seeps in through a crack in the shield that protects her fats. Full of leaf, she clings to a stalk while she is archived in the dark of a machine entirely foreign to the nocturnal foliage she just came to know and the underground vigil of her infancy. She walks two times along the stalk, from top to bottom, though perhaps she sees nothing. She slips but manages to steady herself. Seven times she tries to take off, as if longing for light, but the plastic membrane stops her. Until she seems to resign herself and stops moving. Shits again. Waits.

The light returns, suddenly, when someone opens the refrigerator after a while. Everything begins to shake. The june bug falls to the bottom of the bag but manages to recover from a new round of kicking by clasping to a leaf. She slips and grabs on again many times as the world convulses before coming to rest. Perhaps she feels a sense of calm when the bag is dropped into a basket. Maybe she is blinded by the afternoon sun; if she were free, she would hide from it in a burrow. Everything shudders around her again as the car where they stuck her reaches the unpaved road, which has more potholes in it than usual this rainy season. Though the blazing sun might make her drowsy, it must be impossible to rest while being jostled around with the chard and the bag. When the car hits paved road and the basket stops dancing as much, the beetle, perhaps confused, readies her wings. But again, the plastic blocks any attempt at departure.

No unit of measure could adequately compare the hundred kilometers of winding mountain road smoothed under the car's wheels as it avoids potholes, eighteen-wheelers, and dump trucks with the short trajectory of mud, moss, corpses, and sediment from which the beetle has been exiled. The difference between the energy of the machine that resolutely crosses the cordillera and the tiny zeal in the wings of an insect that asks only for leaves to eat and mud in which to house her eggs. It is hard to find a connection between the five hours it takes the woman driving the car to get to Bogotá and the huge slice of the june bug's two weeks of life that these hours represent. Perhaps displacement resides in these inconceivable connections, in these scandalous imprecisions.

A final shudder rocks the beetle hours later, when the woman removes the chard from the bag in which the june bug is trapped and puts it on the kitchen counter in the apartment that was her destination. The beetle manages to grab a leaf and right herself again before climbing its green surface to discover the call of a new light bulb.

When the beetle takes flight, the woman, who is busy unpacking, doesn't realize for a moment that there's something out of place about that rasping ruckus, that foreign hum. At first, she fails to notice that its purr carries the sonic print of exile and struggles to feel surprised at the beetle's presence in this small apartment in northern Bogotá, where she had never before seen an insect. During the month she spent with her aunt in the countryside, she had gotten used to living with them, though always a bit reluctantly. She swatted away any that tried to land on her head at night while she was reading; in the mornings, she crouched down hundreds of times to save the ones dying belly-up on the patio's paving stones, terrified that she might step on them, and cleared the corpses from the kitchen sink, taken aback that it doubled as a cemetery. But now it is hard for her to admit that the bug flying around her own kitchen comes from the kinked mountains from which she just returned. She wouldn't want to be the one responsible for leaving it orphaned from the dirt. Would it be her fault if the beetle didn't return? She regrets not having a big garden nearby where she could free it. She also wonders if it might be true, what her aunt said about leaving her the finca when she dies. If she were to inherit it, what would she do with all its insects?

The june bug lands on the floor after flirting a while with the dining room lamp. Maybe she is confused by this flat new geography of polished wood and granite with no trace of lumps or clods, where nothing is spongy. The woman grabs her with the slight disgust she now feels at the tickle of insect legs, though she enjoyed it as a child. Perhaps the beetle is surprised by the soft, smooth cave of the woman's palm. And the slippery glass of the empty vase where it deposits her.

If she were still a little girl, she would have slipped the june bug into her pocket without really knowing whether she was searching for company or offering it. Back then, she knew April was April and October was October because of the arrival of flying insects that emerged from the depths and presented themselves in thick clouds, darkening the air and staining gardens brown with their lewd, awkward crunching. At school and in the park down the block, she loved to play with them and let them climb all over her, walking up and down her legs and through the hairs on her arms, certain they were grateful for those paths. She would occasionally stick them in the pockets of her school uniform, pleased with herself for being so generous and sheltering them in her skirt. In fourth grade, she got a one-day suspension for putting dozens of the insects in her desk and then opening the lid to let them fly around the room in the middle of class, just as her teacher was explaining the confusion that can result from the misuse of commas. With few exceptions, all the other students had shrieked in fear and had, from then on, called her gross-out or bug-girl. She secretly loved those nicknames. She was captivated by the temporary company of those nomads who arrived one day, full of enthusiasm, to transform the city's gardens and empty lots with their brief mania for dragging themselves along borders, only to disappear a little while later without any farewell ritual, without anyone lamenting their departure.

But then she grew up and traded rolling around in the grass for homework and phone calls, then it was classes at the university and buses stuck in traffic and boring afternoons in cafés suffering the disquisitions of men who lectured her about things she didn't care about or already knew. And the beetles faded from her days without her noticing. She hadn't needed to mourn them (wasn't that, she thought now, the best goodbye?); when she went to study in Madrid—that dry plateau with its innocuous, unfamiliar insects—she forgot all about those highland bugs and set her sights on bars, mock-ups, blueprints, skin, and ass. Until that December when her aunt invited her to see her new house in the country and she was surrounded by them again. It had surprised her to discover that the devotion she once felt for them no longer existed, that she no longer felt a thrill at the tickling of their prickly legs or tenderness at their clumsy flights. Of all that, she retained only a distant respect, a silent plea not to buzz too close to her. What had changed in her? How could she have closed her heart to them? Was it fair to have abandoned them like that?

She sends a text message to her cousin, a former collector of lizards, crickets, and sometimes beetles, like her. A savior, in her childhood, of dazed butterflies and bees half drowned in puddles. A connoisseur of the roots of radishes, carrots, and grass. They haven't spoken about bugs since they were twelve years old.

> Hey, I'm finally back. How are you? Better, I hope.
>
> Quick question: do you know what happened to the june bugs in Bogotá?
>
> Do you think they still arrive in the rainy season and we just don't see them anymore?
>
> Or did they die out? Or stop coming this way?

It is Saturday, when they usually speak, but her cousin doesn't reply. The windowsill provides no universe for the beetle. But the woman would never be able to toss it in the garbage. When she opens the window, she wonders if it might be best to nudge the bug off the edge, encouraging it to fly to a happier place, to find a garden down below and perhaps stop being a foreigner there. But she fears that the unexpected ten-story drop might startle it, and it might not get its wings ready in time to avoid splattering on the pavement. So she leaves it on the cement that announces the abyss and watches as it lingers, fearless, for a moment. Finally she understands that it is the animal's hermeticism, the armature that renders it both unshakeable and inscrutable, and its total lack of interest in her that horrify her in a way she had sensed before but had not been able to name. How is it not begging for her help? Why does it seem so apathetic and calm? Why isn't it at the ready to fly off, fleeing the captivity she imposed on it? She is tormented by the fact that the june bug seems entirely unconcerned about becoming bait or being deported. That it appears unaware of rifts, the sting of worry, the sadness of goodbye. Or does it feel these things, and she just can't see it? She was better at accepting the mysteries of these creatures when she was a little girl, when she didn't demand answers of them. She didn't know what desires lived inside them but was satisfied with the understanding that they had a secret will unrelated to that of humans, even if she caught them to keep them close. Now a terror blooms in her. She wants to look the bug in the eye but forgets where its eyes are. Wants to persuade it that it's not too late to show the world the distress it must be feeling.

Suspended in a time her armature cultivates with secrecy (a time impossible for us to measure), so foreign to that of the woman returning from vacation, the june bug walks. Smug, perhaps unaware that right beside her is the largest precipice of her brief life.

As she closes the window, the woman vacillates between feeling fearsome and powerful, possessed of an ironclad piety in aid of the defenseless, and writhing with a guilt made of something she can't name. Should she have found it another home? Invited it to live in the dirt of her dead orchid? She decides it would probably be best to avoid getting entangled, especially since there is no way of knowing the desires of the exiled. To accept that there will always be creatures teeming nearby, some of them agonizing, expelled from their days. She turns off the kitchen light and lowers the shade, begging the insect to free itself from those flares and find welcome in one of the gardens below.

Who knows if the beetle, made for combing the earth with antennae and resins, for biting stems and tickling roots, has some kind of compass that allows her to grapple with monumental abysses and avoid the selfish solitude of wall and cement. As she does wherever she falls—as long as she lands right side up—she scratches the ground to keep moving forward. Searching for something to cling to, she stretches her antennae over the gap that swallows her whole. After spinning in the air a few times, she manages to open her wings and slow her descent before landing, clumsily, on the roof of a car. A piece of one diaphanous wing remains outside her shell like a sign of her agitation. She strolls parsimoniously across the smooth steel. When she is just about to slip down the car's windshield, she takes flight again toward a lamp that shines on a rusty sled in the small garden. She circles the light as if she deserved to eat it, until she decides to enter a furrow in the dirt where a few plants battle neglect. She settles on a dried-out lily of the Nile. Perhaps she is searching for the chimera of copulation. How does she ask herself where the others have gone? Who knows how surprised she is by the smell of dirty air that her fanned antennae detect. After a while, she returns to the lamp, as if proving her loyalty to the light, in a back-and-forth that goes from ground to bulb until she lands belly up in the grass. With great effort she manages to stand and head for the garden next door, which is behind a fence. Impossible to guess the outline of her will. Who knows if the crossing feels slow to her. Until she reaches the tall grass of the neighboring house, which is about to be demolished. She clings to the blades to keep herself from tipping over as she ventures farther into the garden, where she finds a dandelion with several rotten leaves. She scratches and chews. She doesn't seem to notice the human hair that has twisted around one of her antennae along the way.

In the morning, after making sure the beetle isn't still on the windowsill requesting accommodation, the woman checks her phone for her cousin's reply.

> Welcome back, cuz! Can u believe I had to work yesterday and ended up in the office until 11? They put me on a housing development in the countryside and it's been nonstop.
>
> It's killing me, I swear.
>
> I'm going to spend all day in bed =) but I'll write later to make a plan so you can tell me how it went at our aunt's
>
> No idea about the june bugs XOX

Only a Little While Here

On her walk to the market, the woman will want to ask the Venezuelans who sometimes sit on the median during their breaks from soliciting loose change if they've seen a june bug circling the lilies. But she will decide that they would see her as either stupid or insensitive, and that they wouldn't be wrong.

By the time the white light that floods Bogotá on cloudy days grows bright enough to be blinding, the june bug has dug herself a refuge in the dirt. Perhaps the rest comes as a relief. As an acquisitive great thrush descends from a lasiandra to make a crunchy feast of the beetle, the woman will be planning her shopping list, checking her email, and paying her electricity bill, which was so long overdue they were about to cut her power. Having already forgotten about all the june bugs in the world, she will be searching for a good chard soup recipe.

It is the first time that the young thrush, hatched just a few months earlier in a rubber tree on a nearby median, has tasted such a large, juicy beetle. It might also be the last. The bird is almost certainly pleased with his catch. His ancestors gobbled up june bugs with zeal twice a year when the insects emerged from the depths to announce that they, too, had a claim on the earth. But perhaps the thrush has no memory of this.

Who knows what it is to be caught in the beak of a hungry bird. Whether the beetle's casing cracks and her legs snap right in that moment, or if she arrives whole and kicking in the thrush's craw. Perhaps she is numbed by the saliva that must stick to her as she rolls along the tunnel that exiles her there.

María Ospina

Until the lava of the bird's stomach melts her valiant resins, dissolves her nomadic strength, and transforms her into a viscous secretion. Certainly the june bug—winged music, forest crackle, witness to the lives of mud—will bequeath some of her vitality to the sharp song of the bird from a city so foreign to her.

IV

Reason for Surrender

To receive a guest in one's home = Zuen vibzasqua
To be received in someone's home = aguem vi izasqua
Perhaps we will meet in another time = fahanga, hac uic aganan chihisty

—Anonymous,
Dictionary and Grammar of the Chibcha Language,
early seventeenth century

The animal is born. faque izasqua

—Anonymous,
Concise Grammar of the Mosca Language (c. 1612)

I lost mountain ranges
where once I slept;
orchards of gold I lost
sweet with life

—Gabriela Mistral, "Country That Is Missing," tr. Langston Hughes

If the at home with oneself of the dwelling is an "at home with oneself as in a land of asylum or refuge," this would mean that the inhabitant also dwells there as a refugee or an exile, a guest and not a proprietor.

—Jacques Derrida, *Adieu: To Emmanuel Levinas*,
tr. Pascale-Anne Brault and Michael Naas

But, of course, the porcupine's cry does not reach us.

—Ida Vitale, *On Plants and Animals*

The porcupine lifts her head when the lid of the box she was stuck in for the journey is raised, and light enters after hours spent suffering the darkness and the jostling of the bus that slammed her relentlessly against the cardboard. Perhaps the air in the room is a relief after being shut away for so long, no matter how aseptic and far removed it is from the lichen-covered bark, the pollen, and the oxidized minerals of what had, until recently, been her home.

She runs her whiskers along the hand of the woman who has raised her since she took her first breath. Perhaps this makes her feel less out of place. Maybe she recognizes the smell of soap and firewood on the woman's skin when she rubs her snout against her fingers, prancing as if desperate to touch the building she was brought to. She waves her tail in the air and finds nothing to curl it around. Who knows if she realized something was about to be lost that cloudless morning when she descended from the croton draco she'd only recently learned to climb and drank her morning milk from the usual stump, only to end up stuck in a dark box. Perhaps the melody of the woman's words from the other side of the cardboard as she told her to stay calm on their way to Bogotá helped her withstand the slamming and bustle of what we would call time (but which must be something else for her).

Maybe when she peers out into the intense light of that room where everything is white and smells of peculiar substances, when she can no longer hear the murmur of other creatures or the collective voice of trees rustling in the wind, or feel the fog come and go, maybe then she will long for the damp world of bark and spongy earth that was all she had known. Where and how does bewilderment settle in her?

"I know the trip was long, but just look how we're here now and you just relax for me all right? Because they're going to take good care of you and they'll feed you good and then they'll let you go again, hear me? They'll take you to some nice mountains where no mean doggies will bother you, nobody will. Not even me."

The woman chuckles and runs a finger over the porcupine's snout, like she always does, until she feels the scratch of the small teeth poking out from the animal's mouth.

"You be patient, hear me?"

The Center's receptionist observes them gravely as she puts on a pair of gloves.

As she does whenever they are together, the porcupine licks the fingers of the woman who pulled her from her mother's womb and has helped her grow ever since. Maybe she is craving the milk that the woman usually gives her in the garden at this hour of the afternoon. As if begging to climb the woman's arm, the porcupine tries to scale one side of the box but only manages to scratch the cardboard with her sharp little claws, which have insisted on growing faster than the rest of her body. Who knows if she senses something like the shock she felt when her mother's heart—which had been pounding harder than ever before as, leaping and shaking, she tried to escape—fell silent as everything went still, and a rift opened in the warm sac that housed her, and she was blinded by light, and someone pulled her once and for all from the body that had protected her. An emergency birth she never asked for.

The porcupine stands on her hind legs again when the receptionist who has taken the box in her latex hands carries her into the next room, which is even brighter than the reception area. She sways her cushiony nose back and forth, as if navigating smells that don't live in any forest—bleach, alcohol, floor cleaner, floral perfumes—and shows more of her teeth still unaccustomed to gnawing. She probably finds the scent of these new hands that refuse to pet her a little strange, having only known those of the woman and her daughter, who feed and care for her.

"Bye now, mamita! You be good, be real patient, all right?"

The porcupine might recognize the voice calling to her from far away but can no longer see the woman. She slides down one of the cardboard walls and rolls when the receptionist sets the box on its side against the opening of a cage, then gets back to her feet and, hesitantly, steps inside what will be her dwelling for a time. A home much smaller than the garden she knew before, which blended with the field and the trees and had no metal bars. She moves slowly, as if the fluorescent lights, too strong for a nocturnal creature like her, were chilling her bones, undoing the few certainties she enjoyed at the edge of a forest in ferment.

The woman wished she could stay longer to explain to the little porcupine that this wasn't a betrayal. That she wasn't abandoning her after taking such good care of her and feeding her with breast milk from her own daughter, who had just given birth. She knows the porcupine wouldn't understand this explanation, or any, but she is certain they will miss each other. She thinks that she should have ignored the advice of the town veterinarian. She senses an injustice, something twisted and cruel in the days or even months that the porcupine will have to spend locked up in the Center before she is assigned a new place to live.

"The poor baby must be dying of thirst. You left some water in her cage? At home she drank loads. I also brought the bottle we always gave her, with milk and all, my daughter's own milk. I'll leave it if you want. She must be just starving after all those buses we had to take to get here. Keep it, please, I don't want her going without her milk."

The receptionist, who is just returning to her desk, looks at her, annoyed.

"Don't worry, we'll take excellent care of her and make sure she gets the right food."

The receptionist adds that the veterinarian will give the

animal a full check-up and establish her optimal diet, which certainly does not include human milk. She explains that they will create an ideal environment for her to adapt while they determine her options for rehabilitation and release.

"But you do think they'll let her out soon? You're not just going to keep her here forever in a cage, because if you are then I'll take her back with me right now, even with how much it cost to get here."

The receptionist explains that if the animal adapts well and has no health issues or illness that might affect its behavior, after a period of observation and confirming that the animal has learned to secure food for itself, they will be able to release it into the wild. That's how she says it, into the wild, and the words sound as strange to the woman as if they had come from the inner crust of another world.

"I remember when some people from here, from the Department of Environmental Protection, that's you, right? When you came to the community where I live with some doctors and some military guys to release an eagle, a black-chested eagle, you know the ones I mean? Beautiful animals. So dignified. They said they confiscated her in Bogotá, from a pet store. Can you believe it? That they didn't know what part of the country she'd been stolen from but since they're the kind that live way up in the mountains, like where I'm from, well. Imagine the cruelty. They released her in my neighbor's field and she took off for the mountains, happy as can be."

"It's nice that you care so much about animals."

"You should have seen that eagle flying toward those cliffs. So fast, so glad to be free, finally, after being shut in for so long. Imagine. It was so beautiful to see her up there, I'll never forget it as long as I live."

The receptionist is focused on the computer and asks for a few minutes to locate the right forms so they can proceed with the requisite paperwork for the surrender.

"It was like the mountain was calling the eagle to it. We call that one Muiba, and it's where they say the Indians all jumped from when they were being chased by the Spanish, because they would rather die than live as their slaves. A powerful mountain, a magical one, they say. People say you see things up there. Especially the older folk. My grandma always said. I know it's true, but I haven't seen anything, myself. I think that eagle's still alive. God willing, may she live happily ever after up there with nobody to bother her. I saw her flying way up high some time ago now, near the mountain closest to my house. Must have been going to hunt, with all the little creatures that live up there and all. But I haven't seen her since. That was around when my daughter got pregnant, that is, a year ago. Must have gone off somewhere."

The receptionist looks through papers in a folder.

"That's why I believe you when you say you'll take good care of my little baby and let her go free again soon, right? You give me your word?"

"Yes, of course. Don't worry. Just one moment and I'll take your information down and we can finish with this paperwork so you can go."

"That's why I didn't want to leave her with the police in town, why I wanted to bring her here. When the vet told me that I could be fined for keeping a wild animal in my house, that it's against the law, well of course I got scared. I don't want anyone thinking I stole her, not when what I did was save her when her momma died, may she rest in peace, and then that vet saying I would get in trouble with the law for raising her."

"I'm just waiting for a few details from the doctor and then I can take your report and we can put all this in there."

The woman straightens up a bit to peer through the windows into the next room, where they took the porcupine, but she doesn't see her.

The porcupine drinks some water and drags her snout across the hay on the floor of her cage, as if trying to find the spongy layer of leaves and grass she was used to crossing. It is hard to know if the stillness is comforting after being jostled around, or if the whirring of machines and buzz of the lights disorients her further. She walks in circles inside the cage, perhaps looking for food. Curls her fidgety tail around the metal bars. Tilts her head upward, occasionally, as if looking for the grown tree she deserves. She seems to be using her snout to inspect the whole room, where nothing is rough and everything screams of symmetry. Who knows if she catches sight of the squirrel monkey in the other corner of the room, searching endlessly for the best way to hang from the bars of his cage, or the wood fox biting one of the claws on his forepaw and occasionally looking over at her (maybe wanting to eat her). Do they wonder where their mountain went, as she perhaps does? Do they all exude the musk of being stuck in the wrong corner?

The woman sits in the reception area while the veterinarian checks the animal to fill out the mandatory surrender paperwork. Everything seems so organized and new, so clean, much more so than any office she's ever been in, either in town or here in Bogotá. She examines the glass doors marked ARRIVALS—ZONE 1, where they took the porcupine, and ARRIVALS—ZONE 2, where several cages hang from the ceiling. She catches a glimpse of four parakeets in one and a macaw in another. Near the receptionist, there is a poster with the image of several yellow-crowned parrots peeking out from holes bored into a palm tree and the words: IT'S A TREAT TO SEE AN ANIMAL IN THE WILD! RESPECT THEM AND KEEP THEIR HABITAT HEALTHY. #FREEATHOME and another with a picture of a monkey climbing a tree that reads ARE YOU AN ACCOMPLICE TO ANIMAL TRAFFICKING? IN COLOMBIA, IT IS ILLEGAL TO TRAP, SELL, OR REMOVE WILD ANIMALS. #FREEATHOME. On another wall, a table with a list of animals to which the woman imagines her companion will be added.

<u>ADMITS / COUNT (NOVEMBER)</u>
Red-footed tortoise 3
Pond slider turtle 28
Blue and yellow macaw 2
Brown-throated parakeet 4
Squirrel monkey 9
Tufted capuchin 3
Cobalt-rumped parrotlet 2
Orange-chinned parakeet 7
Lined seedeater 1
Tarantula (var. spec.) 194
Scorpion 17
Dart frog (golden) 216
Green iguana 2
Wood fox 1

On the screen of a muted television, men in suits and ties greet each other on a stage. The audience applauds. Then the image of an army helicopter shooting into the rain forest, and people in camouflage standing in line to turn over their weapons. The words scrolling below read: SECOND ANNIVERSARY OF THE PEACE ACCORD BETWEEN THE GOVERNMENT AND FARC GUERRILLAS. Several men in ties give interviews, and the woman recognizes one as the president. Then, farmers working the land, followed by a female news anchor and the image of a fat man in handcuffs above the words LEADER OF THE BLACK EAGLES EXTRADITED TO THE UNITED STATES. The woman thinks about one of her nephews, paid to fight as part of a counter-guerrilla military operation in Catatumbo these past five years, and wonders how much longer he'll be there.

The porcupine tries to stand on her hind legs when a man in white approaches her cage, as if wanting to nuzzle him. Perhaps she thinks he is going to feed her, since she didn't get her afternoon milk. Or maybe she just wants to get out of there. But the bars are thin and too smooth for her fingers, which are accustomed to rough bark, and she slips. She forces her nose through and sniffs the man who has come to study her. Her whiskers, longer than her head, weave between the bars and touch the leather gloves there to examine her. She climbs the veterinarian's arm when he opens her cage, as if she were grateful to hold on to something living, as if when they took her from her mother she accepted that any human hand could save her. Perhaps the man's deep voice seems strange to her, accustomed as she is to living among women. She rubs her nose on the white lab coat, which gives off a scent of disinfectant, a smell she has surely never encountered before. When the man pushes back from her face the brown hairs where her yellow quills are beginning to come in, she opens her mouth, as if trying to frighten him with her teeth. Do her whiskers hurt when they're tugged? She coils her tail harder against the man's arm while he examines her eyes and snout with a flashlight. She probably finds the table she is then placed on inhospitable, cold and smooth as it is. Perhaps she is unsettled by the scratch of metal against her claws. When the man flips her over to inspect her abdomen and study her flesh, she tries to wriggle upright. Maybe she is surprised by how forcefully he holds her, since no one has ever examined her like that, illuminating the deepest caverns sheltered by her thick coat. She kicks when he palpates her teats, bends the joints of her legs, spreads her toes, and inspects her anus. She attempts to wrap her tail around his hand, as if refusing to submit. She seems to resist when he tries to open her mouth, but she can't prevent his determined fingers from working her jaws apart to explore inside.

The woman notices that the receptionist has gone to speak with the veterinarian in Zone 1. It makes her sad that they didn't let her say a proper goodbye, that they just took the porcupine away all of a sudden, not acknowledging the special bond between them. She is haunted by the thought of the little one missing the smells of her kitchen and the garden full of blackberries, the moss on the trees, warm milk, her and her daughter's voices, and the mist. She wonders again if it was a good decision to bring her there. Again she feels the bitterness that ran her through the day her dog killed the porcupine's mother and thinks how everything would be different if she were still alive. The two porcupines would be sniffing around the mountain, climbing trees, munching on berries and fruits from the higuerón, avoiding owls at night. That little one shouldn't be displaced and at the mercy of so many people.

Will she get her daily milk? Will she suffer when they wean her? Will anyone there talk to her as sweetly as she did?

When the receptionist returns to the front desk, she hands the woman a note.

Coendou vestitus: brown hairy dwarf porcupine

The receptionist explains that those are the scientific name and the common name for the animal; the veterinarian had asked her to say that their natural habitat is the highland forests of the Andes, that is, where the woman lives, and that the species is considered vulnerable to extinction.

"So thank you for bringing her in, because there's not many of these little creatures left and we have to protect them."

The receptionist adds that the center has already rehabilitated two of these porcupines and was able to release them without any problem.

"Well, you let the doctor know there's a whole bunch out where I live."

"I only mention it so you know we have experience with porcupines. You don't need to worry, the animal is in good hands."

The woman thinks about how strange the first name looks. *Coendou vestitus*. She guesses it must be in English. She imagines a dress covered in spikes that someone might wear to a party full of gringos.

"Tell the doctor and everyone who's going to take care of her to be really careful with her quills. I don't know if you saw them, they're yellow and black and they'll get longer as she grows. You saw how they're coming in, right?"

"I didn't, ma'am. But I'm sure the doc already made a note of it."

"Porcupines' quills are living things, you know, and if they get in your skin they just love to go deep in there in a hurry, faster than you'd think, and then you can't get them out again. In old times, they said that if one of those spikes stays in you too long, the porcupine that stuck you takes over your life. If something bad happens to the porcupine, or if it feels pain, then the person feels it too. If the porcupine dies, the person will get sick and die too. Please tell the doctors that, if you don't mind."

"Of course, don't worry, I'll tell them."

"Listen, we got pretty attached to her and I wasn't sure it was a good idea to bring her here, for her I mean, but in the end what made up my mind was that she's starting to grow quills and my grandson is about start crawling all around and I don't want them playing and him getting hurt."

The assistant indicates to the woman that she is ready to go over the questions on the surrender form.

THE OFFICE OF THE MAYOR OF BOGOTÁ D.C.
DEPARTMENT OF ENVIRONMENTAL PROTECTION
DIVISION: FORESTRY, WILD FLORA AND FAUNA
SUBDIVISION: WILD FAUNA
CERTIFICATE OF VOLUNTARY SURRENDER OF SPECIMEN(S): No. 947

GENERAL INFORMATION ON SURRENDER

Date of surrender:	Address of surrender:
24 November 2018	Center for the Care and Assessment of Wild Flora and Fauna, Bogotá

Name of individual surrendering animal:	**Identification:**
Teresa Tibaquirá Ruiz	cc 45.376.908

Address:	**Telephone:**
Vereda El Silencio, Miscua county, Boyacá (no exact address)	311-297-1135

Received by:
Aura Janeth Ramos Aguilar, Administrative Assistant, Registration, CCAWFF Bogotá

Reason for surrender:
The woman surrendering the specimen indicates that approximately one and a half months ago her dog killed a porcupine near her home and she saw something moving in the corpse's abdomen and thought the animal might be pregnant, at which point she performed a cesarean section on the animal with a knife and removed the specimen she is here to surrender, identified as a *Coendou vestitus*, brown hairy dwarf porcupine. She indicates that the animal seemed ready to be born when she removed it, and that it reacted well and took the milk she offered from her daughter, who has a four-month-old baby. They have given the animal breast milk all this time, at first with a spoon, then resently they have been using a small baby bottle and the animal has no problem with it. The woman says it has always had a big appetite and it's twice as big now as when it was born and that it climbs trees now and looks for berries but it still drinks the milk, that it's very docile and took a liking to the woman and her daughter, it can come and go from the house when it wants

and the dog leaves it alone, even though it killed its mother. The reason for surrender is that a veterinarian gave her the information of the CCAWFF and told her it is illegal to keep wild animals in captivity and also because she isn't sure she can take care of it much longer because she's looking for work and she wouldn't want to leave it out there on the mountain unless she was sure it could survive on its own, she asks that we return this specimen to the area where she lives because she says there are many similar animals there.

DESCRIPTION OF SURRENDERED SPECIMEN(S):

Scientific name	Condition	Quantity	Sex
Coendou vestitus	Pending evaluation	1	Female

GENERAL HISTORY OF LIVING SPECIMEN(S):

Place of origin	Manner of acquisition
Vereda El Silencio, Miscua county, Boyacá	Specimen was not acquired, see reason for surrender
Site of acquisition	**Time in possession of specimen**
Specimen found in Vereda El Silencio, Miscua county, Boyacá (no exact address)	37 days

Presence of other animals:
Species endemic to the upper forests of the Eastern Andes. On the farm where the specimen was born there were chickens, a sheep, a cat, and a dog (individual surrendering the specimen states that all animals are current on vaccinations).

Previous diet:
From birth the specimen was fed human breast milk, the individual reports that during the previous two and a half weeks the animal has learned to eat berries from the trees but continues to consume human milk.

Condition:
No evidence of abuse, initial veterinary exam confirms that the animal is in good condition.

Illness or treatments:
Preliminary veterinary examination indicates no illness at the time of surrender, pending full exam etc.

OBSERVATIONS
Time of arrival: 2:48pm
Hospitalization: No
Profile/Biological History (mammals) No. 1387
Additional observations:
Veterinary exam in Arrivals conducted by Fr. Guáqueta Rodríguez Ángel David.
The individual surrendering the animal asked to be informed when the animal is returned to its natural habitat. She has been informed about current laws regarding the possession and illegal trafficking of wild animals.

BY SURRENDERING THE AFOREMENTIONED SPECIMEN(S) AND SIGNING BELOW, I AFFIRM THAT I WILL NOT PURCHASE OR GIVE AS A GIFT OR KEEP AS A PET ANY OTHER WILD ANIMAL.

NAMES AND SIGNATURES

Aura Janeth Ramos Aguilar Administrative Assistant Registration, CCAWFF Bogotá **Name and signature of CCAWFF representative**	Teresa Tibaquirá Ruiz **Name and signature of individual surrendering specimen(s)**

Department of Environmental Protection
Av. Caracas No. 54-38, Bogotá D.C. Colombia, PBX: 3778899
www.ambientebogota.gov

The woman looks over the form she is being asked to sign.

"You could also put there that I didn't want to leave her with the local police because they would probably have left her to die in a box right there in their office. I really wouldn't put it past them. I knew it was going to cost a lot to bring her here, it's not easy, you know, but I wasn't going to leave her there."

"Don't worry, ma'am, the most important part is already in the report."

"Do you think you could let me say goodbye to her, miss?"

"I'm so sorry, ma'am, but once the animal is inside, we're not allowed to bring it back out. Soon the animal will get its full veterinary examination, and then, if it doesn't require any further intervention, it will go into quarantine until it's ready for maintenance and rehabilitation, which is where they make a special area for it to learn the behaviors it will need in the wild before it is released. Don't worry, everything will be fine."

The woman remembers when her mother was hospitalized in Tunja, dying of stomach cancer, and she had to beg at the reception desk to be let in to see her.

"And how long do you think they'll keep her here before releasing her, if you would be so kind?"

"They'll release the animal when rehabilitation is complete, if they decide that release is the best course of action. But if you want my opinion, I'm no veterinarian, but I've been working here for three years and I've seen lots of these little guys rehabilitated. I think they'll release yours because of how young it is, and I'll bet it can still learn what it needs to survive in the wild. When they come in that young, it's almost always a happy ending."

"I hope it doesn't take too long."

Impatient, the assistant indicates that she has taken down all the woman's information and the experts will decide whether to release the animal nearby.

"And there's no way you could call me when they finally release her? Just for my peace of mind. Even if they take her somewhere else, I'd just like to know that she's in a forest again."

"Like I said, I can't make any promises, but I included your request in the report. We'll just have to wait and see."

"It's just that I got pretty fond of her. Do me the favor. Please, miss."

The assistant avoids the woman's eyes and types something on her computer.

"If I hear anything, I'll do my best to call and let you know. You can count on it. Now, if you'll just sign here, you can go."

The woman signs and marks with her fingerprint both copies of the printed form. It doesn't seem fair that she's being asked to promise never to trap or traffic wild animals, as if she were a kidnapper stealing creatures from the mountain for profit.

She would like to tell the assistant that no one protects the forests near her home more than she does, which is why she decided to become the president of her local community board, and that she confronted a few of her neighbors who wanted to chop down trees even though it isn't allowed, and that if it weren't for people like her, there wouldn't be any oncillas or squirrels or porcupines or eagles, or all those other birds. But she senses that she'd better not annoy the assistant if she wants her to keep her promise. So she says nothing and sticks her signed copy into her backpack. She feels a rift opening between the solid, fleshy, furry weight of the porcupine she cared for so dearly and the inert paper she was handed. When she returns home, she will place it in a drawer with all the other documents that have been softened and stained by the fog-loving mildew. Where she also keeps a wad of cash, her grandmother's rosary, a gold-plated ring left to her by her mother, the piece of Indigenous pottery and the stone shaped into an axe head that she found on the mountain as a girl, and her bag of family photos. She thinks about how she will fold a few yellow-and-black quills from the porcupine's mother, which she pulled by the head from her dog's muzzle and laid out to dry, into that paper that pained her so much to sign. She wishes she had something from the baby, even just one of the little quills starting to come in now, to store with the others as a keepsake.

"If you'd be so kind, tell her I love her and that she should be brave. That maybe we'll see her again, but that if not, we'll never forget her. Tell her that."

The porcupine seems to want to cling to the man's arm when he tries to put her back in her cage after finishing her physical examination and starting to fill out her profile. She struggles to climb higher, as if there were a succulent berry on his head, or as if all the branches awaiting her forever were growing there at once. The man praises her, carefully unclenches her arms, unwraps her clinging tail, and places her inside. She circles around in the hay, scratching her whiskers against the dry stalks. Maybe the smell reminds her a little of the grass around her house. But in the world of that cage there is no humidity cloaking the mud, no moss, no patient leaves that climb and later offer themselves to the earth. She digs in it with her powerful claws until she scratches the newspaper underneath. Perhaps she finds the smell of ink entirely foreign to the vapors and ferments of her original home. She uses her whiskers to take in the dry, sterile ground that might communicate nothing to her. She might be tired and hungry. Will she be able to sleep there during the day, as she deserves? Will she long for breast milk and tree bark? Will she miss the woman?

V

When the Dog Howls and the Bird Cries

Believest thou in dreams?
At which hour doth cry the turtledove 'r howl the dog,
think'st thou some terrible thing shall befall?
[...]
Vm Muysua o casaqy vm guquá?
Sumgiu, to, ainnân ipquã tabê ghaica
mhas aqy niû ybas guy vmgàguâ

> —Fray Bernardo de Lugo, *Grammar in the General Language of the New Kingdom of Granada, Called Mosca* (1619)

To recognize that the world is a space of immersion means, on the contrary, that there are no real or stable frontiers: the world is the space that never lets itself be reduced to a house, to what is one's own, to one's digs, to the immediate. Being in the world means to exercise influence especially outside one's own home, outside one's own habitat, outside one's own niche. It is always the totality of the world one lives in, which is and will always be infested by others.

> —Emanuele Coccia, *The Life of Plants*, tr. Dylan Montanari

Then practice losing farther, losing faster:
places, names, and where it was you meant
to travel. None of these will bring disaster.

> —Elizabeth Bishop, "One Art"

Kati and Mona

Kati and Mona wake up earlier than usual when the man who has been caring for them over the past few months at the Animal Care Unit reaches their cell. They rise, without pausing to stretch, ready to shower him with affection in the form of leaps and licks. Even before he opens the door to let them gallop along the corridor and head out to roll around in the courtyard, he senses that it will be the last time they are together. He ties a blue handkerchief around each of their necks. Mona doesn't seem to mind how the fabric, which reads BOGOTÁ LOVES ANIMALS, hugs the fronds of her neck and musses her brown mantle. She licks the man's forearm with the same trust as always, and for the first time, he feels like he is betraying her. Kati is annoyed and lowers her head, sinking under the weight of the kerchief, as if it were an iron helmet. Maybe she remembers being spayed months earlier, just a few days after she arrived at the shelter, and how she had spent several days in a plastic cone and a state of stupefaction.

"Come on, now, don't be stubborn. You look beautiful."

He wishes he could ease her indignation, but he knows she is headstrong and rebellious.

In the corridor, Kati rubs her coat against the bars of the other cells, battling the euphoria that rocks her every time they let her out, determined to shred the submission they have draped over her. Perhaps she remembers the small hours when she would buck in circles around their cart in the park, half playfully and half defiantly, when Luis would squeeze her into a sweater to protect her from freezing temperatures overnight. Maybe the defiant streak she cultivated in the street, which was stifled when the police came and the bulldozers razed her home, is finally returning.

Kati and Mona are the last to reach the sunny courtyard where the dogs are getting fresh air that Saturday morning. Perhaps they're startled by the reggaeton blasting for the first time from recently installed speakers, drowning out the barks of some of the other dogs at play. They both seem happy to see the others reveling, contentedly sniffing each other's asses, tussling on the cement, and recognizing each other from the folds of their flesh. As is their habit, Mona follows Kati to the far corner of the garden, where the guayacán tree is. She pees into the puddle the other has just expelled. Then she returns to the cement, which is just warming up with the sun, and sits back on her hips with her hind legs in the air to carefully lick her vulva until one of the new puppies launches himself at her, begging to play. As always, Kati heads for the shadows all the way in the back, where grass climbs eagerly over everything, to sniff the courtyard wall. She sticks her muzzle in a hole to catch whatever is floating out in the street; after so many months in that place, she must know it all well. Maybe on Saturdays, with less human zeal on the other side, the life filtering through that worn wall smells different. The aroma of empanadas from the cart on the corner surely must reach her. The trash a stray dog spread across the street a few days earlier and no one has swept away. The air, a bit thinner. Maybe the smell of fried food, dust, and sewage that seeps in from outside reminds her of her days with Luis, when they would collect leftovers from the shops downtown. Or maybe not, which doesn't mean she isn't thinking of him at other times.

Despite the agitation of the other dogs, neither Kati nor Mona seems interested in the new people entering the courtyard. Dozens of strangers oozing the desire to save a homeless animal. Who knows what nervous curiosity smells like (if it has a smell) when mixed with soap and detergent, and whether those vapors assault a wet nose or two.

A woman who has just arrived studies Kati as she returns from the far end of the courtyard to the cement where the others are rolling around. She examines her trot. She likes the dog's insistence on poking around the margins. She has always been suspicious of ones that are too eager to please and doesn't want to end up with a submissive dog that will beg relentlessly for her affection. In the distance, Kati lies down and arches her back with her paws in the air, delighting alone in some mystery. The woman loves that Kati is so self-possessed and nearly catches from her a desire to dance.

She had originally wanted to adopt a retired police dog. One of those proud Labradors or German shepherds she had seen so often on the news, puffing out their chests beside recently seized shipments of drugs, or sniffing their way through fields where roots and fungi embrace explosives and decomposing bodies. She had heard on those same news programs that the police put them up for adoption after they reached a certain age or completed a certain number of missions. After retiring from the bank and buying a country cabin in Boyacá from her cousin, she decided that she needed to share the land with an animal that brave. She didn't fully understand her need to feel—in a clear, concrete way—the fundamental goodness of things; to prove that redemption could exist in a world that seemed so full of hostility. She was ready to explain to anyone who asked, or didn't, that her new home was in an area where the war was a thing of the past. She wouldn't mention the graffiti in a nearby town praising the paramilitary—that had been years ago. She wouldn't say that there had been guerrilla fighters camped in the distant valleys she could see from her house, and that some time ago there had been a confrontation with emerald smugglers.

When she had arrived at the adoption event for police dogs one week before meeting Kati at the shelter—late, like she was late to everything—the last two had just been spoken for. The officer she spoke with told her that these adoption events always drew a big crowd because people admired the dogs for their contributions to society. That was how he said it: their contributions to society, and she had nodded, even as she knew that the phrase concealed something terrible, the nightmare of detecting illegal chemicals and fetid odors and the pain caused by war, under the orders of police officers all too glad to be in command of something. He had advised her to get to the next adoption event early, since sometimes up to thirty-five people lined up for the chance to take home a few of these canine heroes. That was how he said it: canine heroes, and she had thought that she'd never heard that combination of words before, but that he was right. The man, who spoke as if the dogs were his children, explained that the prosecutor's office had between ninety and one hundred trained dogs, that the police had another fifty, and that ten were retired every year. That they organized a special ceremony, and each animal was given a medal for their service. Among the accomplished dogs that were adopted that morning, one had detected 250 corpses during her eight years searching for mass graves in Antioquia and had found another 123 bodies buried in Meta. Two others were famous for all the shipments of cocaine they had discovered during the years they worked in airports in Bogotá and Medellín. There was even a rumor that some drug lord had put a price on the head of one dog who was especially good at her job, Diva, so they kept a security detail on her, as if she were a politician whenever she went out on duty. Another was an expert at identifying currency and had spent years sniffing out fortunes behind walls and in the false bottoms of suitcases. The last one had been retired early after losing several digits when he found bodies in a Buenaventura hideout that had been dissolved in chemicals; he had gotten some of the corrosive substance on his paws. The woman was saddened not to be able to offer one of these dogs a thick forest where he or she could use their nose in a different way, where the earth would offer them foliage and woodland creatures, not addictive dust, nitroglycerin, or human flesh burnt by acid. She wondered if the body of a torture victim smelled the same as the bones of a squirrel or a mouse or a lizard.

When she called the Animal Care Unit after her failed attempt with the canine heroes, she was told that at the upcoming adoption event she had heard about on the radio she would be able to take home a dog that had been dewormed, spayed or neutered, and microchipped. Chosen by her. Photocopy of her identification, proof of address, interview with a member of the staff, and a minimum donation of $50,000 pesos if she belonged to income tier three or above, which she did. At the shelter, she would be able to choose from dogs of all different sizes and backgrounds. Dogs that had been lost, abandoned, or returned; strays brought in off the street and puppies born in Animal Care. The woman waited a week, hoping to find a big, robust one without shaggy fur or an underbite, and that most definitely didn't have a chihuahua face or a pom-pom tail. A dog like the ones she always admired in silence when she saw them cross Carrera Séptima near her apartment. Dignified and self-possessed. Sovereign and strong.

A few nights before going to the adoption event at the shelter, the woman watched a news story about a man who lived on the street in Ciudad Bolívar with eleven dogs that he had invited to join him in the abandoned lot where he had built a little shack from scraps. He adored them and took good care of them, but the police went in to destroy his home and the homes he had built for the dogs out of cardboard and planks. A neighbor captured on video a police officer screaming at the man to get out of there, saying that he would burn the whole place to the ground if he saw him there again. Several women from the neighborhood got together to rebuild the structures using better materials and started collecting funds for the man and his dogs. They live on our block, this is their home, and we don't have any problem with them, one woman said. A veterinarian stated that the animals were in excellent health and that Mr. Rodríguez clearly took very good care of them. Having a dog is not a right only for the privileged, he said. Social Services looked into helping the man find a place to live with his animals and getting them spayed and neutered. Mr. Rodríguez said, I'm not going anywhere because this is where we live and I just want to take care of my dogs, then he added that he made an honest living as a recycler and that the dogs were his family. The camera showed several of the dogs, surrounding him and lovingly licking his cheeks. The woman had nearly cried. She immediately wanted to donate to the cause but didn't know where to send the money, and her internet search produced no leads. She sent the news program an email asking to be put in touch with the reporter who had covered the story. Her doubts about adopting a dog vanished that night. When she turned off the television, she thought to herself that it was a sign. A calling. It made her happy to hear her niece's congratulations over the phone when she confirmed her intention.

On the morning of the adoption event at the Animal Care Unit, the woman got up early to buy a bag of dog treats (bacon flavored) before driving to what in her youth was called the city pound. She was nervous, and while stopped at a red light halfway there, she considered turning around. When she was a little girl, the family dog, Linda, ran away during a birthday party after someone left the door open, and she had secretly cried for nights on end thinking about that terrifying place where dogs that had been picked up off the street were electrocuted. But she knew, from her niece and from a news report she had seen on television, that the city no longer allowed animals collected from the streets to be put down, and that they were all up for adoption. Her niece, who had adopted two cats, had promised her that the animals were treated well at the shelter, and that she would find one that wasn't traumatized.

Mona doesn't realize that someone has kidnapped her friend. She is busy playing with a puppy that arrived a few weeks earlier and is rubbing against her hind leg, as if rebelling against his recent castration. She seems to enjoy wrestling with the little one, tossing him around with her big paws as if she were going to crush him, though she never does.

When the man took Kati and Mona from their cage that morning, he promised himself that if one of them got adopted, he would make sure they got to say goodbye. But there are so many people waiting, and he is busy showing several families the youngest puppies. He doesn't realize that someone has taken Kati to the registration desk, where a woman is looking her over.

Kati bites the leash they've slipped around her neck and resists the tugging of the veterinary assistant, as if she sensed the avalanche of human exuberance filling the courtyard and would prefer the solitude of her playtime. Or maybe she remembers when the men from Animal Care caught her.

The woman likes that she is high-spirited because she believes it to be a sign of intelligence. She is relieved that she doesn't need to worry about how the animal can't walk on a leash, since at her new home in the countryside she will have no reason to limit her movement. Kati tries to pull away, but the woman approaches her and scratches the fine hairs behind her ears, the place she loves to pet dogs when she is agitated, to calm herself down. There is something about the smoothness of Kati's head, in her proud curiosity as she stares into the distance, that convinces the woman she is the one. She is surprised when the dog wriggles free of her hand, then runs her muzzle up her leg and into her groin to smell her ass.

"And what do we know about this beautiful girl?"

"We call her Lady. She probably had an owner, but we don't know for sure because we found her on the street. When she arrived six months ago, she showed no signs of physical trauma and was very well fed. She had a teeny bit of mange on her back, but we treated her right away and she's perfectly fine now. The veterinarians estimate she's around two and a half, but she might be a little older."

"And she won't turn out to be traumatized?"

"I won't lie to you, she was really sad when she first arrived. But, in our experience, that's perfectly normal. Even dogs that come to us straight from wealthy homes. Just imagine—I don't think any of us would do so well with being abandoned. But she adjusted well, and she's happy now. All the other dogs respect her—adore her, actually—especially the one she shares a kennel with. She's somewhere around here too, I can show her to you, if you like. The two of them are inseparable."

"But who do you think she lived with before? You can't tell me for sure whether she was a stray?"

The assistant says that the only thing they can guarantee is that she has been in excellent health the entire time she has been there. The woman thinks to herself that Lady is a terrible name and decides to change it right away.

ANIMAL CARE UNIT, BOGOTÁ D.C.
AGENCY FOR THE PROTECTION AND WELL-BEING OF ANIMALS
ADOPTION SURVEY

Name and identification: *Gloria Inés Rengifo, c.c. 4975125346*

1. **Reason for wanting to adopt a dog:**
   Love for all the animals in the world.

2. **Have you adopted a dog before?**
   A few years ago, I took in a friend's dog when she moved to Argentina and couldn't take the dog with her. She was five at the time, and I cared for her until he died at ten. We had five good years together. I don't know if this information is useful, but maybe so.

3. **Do you have, or have you had, other dog(s) before? Please describe each case:**
   4 dogs in the past 25 years (approximately). I don't know if this counts, but I grew up around dogs my whole life, so the list might get pretty long. Right now I have a ten-month-old boxer named Thief, he's been with me since he was a puppy.

4. **Do you have any animals in your care other than dogs at this time?**
   Two months ago, a cat showed up and I adopted it, but I'm not sure it counts as my pet because my neighbor, who is now my housekeeper, feeds it at her house, so I never see it anymore. But I know it's fine and is up-to-date on vaccines.

   If you answered yes to questions 3 or 4, are your pets up-to-date on their vaccinations? Are they dewormed and seen regularly by a veterinarian?
   Of course, always. Now that I live in the country, I take my dog to the town vet for his vaccinations and all the rest.

5. **Where will the canine live?**
   Finca Nubes, Vereda El Silencio, Miscua county, Boyacá (El Silencio is a rural community, so there's no street address).

6. **Type of residence and outdoor spaces the dog will have access to:**
   A house in the countryside on ten hectares of meadows and forest, the dog will be able to roam wherever she wants.

7. **Where will the animal spend most of its time? Please be specific:**
   She'll live outside, but her bed will be on a covered patio that she'll share with my other dog, Thief. I will probably let her inside the house too, depending on how she adapts.

8. **How many hours will the dog spend outside each day?**
   Most of the day. If it rains, there are places to take shelter on the patio, and there's a roof over their beds.

9. **How many hours will the dog spend alone each day?**
   She will always have the company of my other dog, and I promise they'll get along well because he's very calm. I also live out there full-time now, so I will be with them during the day, and when I have to travel, my neighbor, who is now my housekeeper, can always take care of them. She's great with animals. So the answer is never.

10. **Finish this sentence: The most important thing is that my pet . . .**
    Keeps me company, has a home, and is happy.

    Thank you!
    Thank you so much, and you're welcome.

The woman almost can't get her new companion into the back of her car because Kati refuses to get into the second machine trying to tear her from her days. Straining, the woman manages to set her front paws onto the floor and clumsily lift her hind legs, frustrated with the strength she has lost over the past few years despite decades of Pilates. Kati wriggles like an enormous worm before collapsing on her side onto a pile of newspapers. Rattled, she gets to her feet, trying to recover her dignity.

"There you go, that's a good girl. Good. You're going to love your new life, you'll see."

It feels strange to speak to a dog like that, she never did it with any of her other dogs, but she thinks it might ease the transition. She pets her, relieved that she isn't trying to bite her (if she were a dog, she thinks, she would at least bare her teeth). The woman is surprised that Kati isn't trying to escape and understands when she rejects the bacon-scented treat she is offered. When she growls softly in reply.

Kati is panting. She stares at a point that seems to exist somewhere behind the woman's body. Impossible to know if she wonders where she is being taken. She arches her torso in an even more crooked curve, pulling her heart away, as if in that position she might better endure this new shock. She seems like a badly taxidermized creature. Her panting is no longer the breath of playtime or a fan when she is drowsy from the heat. It might be her unease at the injustice of how others try to erode her pride and her strength. She shoots her breath out quickly, just like she did in the van that exiled her from downtown Bogotá six months earlier, when she met her Mona. Maybe today she remembers the smell of that abduction.

Mona

When he realizes that Kati isn't hovering around the edges of the courtyard, the man who has been looking after them for months goes to find Mona, whom he has named Reina. She is rolling around in the grass, shaking out the raw joy that invades her on sunny mornings. Someone might think she was moving to the rhythm of the reggaeton blasting from the speakers, a famous song he knows by heart, though this time he doesn't feel able to hum along with the singer's conviction that abandonment is trivial and only temporary. *Si conmigo te quedas o con otro tú te vas no me importa un carajo porque sé que volverás.* The lines repeat, but no one seems to pay much attention to their promise of return, or its fissures.

When they first arrived at the shelter, Kati and Mona were always together in the courtyard. As if some bond had been forged between them the first time they rubbed the dew of their noses onto one another and bumped their tails. Over time, though, the man noticed that even if that bond was still tight in their cell, they had started distancing themselves from one another outside, as if they were seizing the opportunity to sniff things beyond each other's oils and breath. Now he knows where the one is who loves to play with the puppy, but he can't find the other anywhere. The assistant confirms that she was just adopted.

"Lady barely let herself be walked out of here, crazy little mutt. I'm just so glad the woman wanted her for a house out in the country. Can you believe the luck?"

She is in the middle of playing, but Mona lets the man put a leash on her and follows him obediently across the office, where several families are filling out adoption forms. Near the street, past the bars that mark the edge of the Animal Care Unit's parking lot, there's nothing to be seen but cars, an open fruit shop, and people walking. The dog from the hardware store across the street sticks his head out; Mona sees him and wags her tail, and he barks back at her. The woman from the empanada stand says she doesn't know who's come out that way because she's had a lot of customers. The man bends in half, partly to hug Mona, and partly because his shame is crushing him, and he doesn't know how to tell her that her captivity is about to become even more painful.

"Don't worry, mamita, you'll find a good home and you'll be really happy there. It won't be long, you'll see. Maybe even today. I promise. Trust me, I'll do everything I can."

Mona seems to like it when he rubs the freckled skin of her belly where her nipples peek out, and she throws herself to the ground so he can scratch her better.

"And Lady will remember you always. You can bet on it."

His voice cracks when he tries to tell her that they both

have good memories and there's no way either will forget all they've been through together. He decides against saying anything and thinks of how his mother used to yell at him when he was little for crying. He thinks about the black lapdog he looked after in the shelter a few years earlier; a family took him home only to return him six months later with his spirit broken, unraveling from within. He wonders if the same thing will happen to Lady.

Mona looks at him, appearing a bit confused about why they are standing for the first time at the edge of a street she must know from the smells that reach the courtyard, but that she has never seen before. Does she remember the grief that overcame her outside the park where she was abandoned by the woman who had raised her? She runs her tongue along the freshly shaved cheek of her caretaker, who is kneeling to pet her, just like she used to do with the people in her home. Maybe she senses his sadness and guilt and wants to ease his sorrows. Defeated, he returns with her to Animal Care, thinking that he should adopt her but not knowing how he could manage to keep a dog that big in the studio apartment he shares with his aunt. It pains him to anticipate how he will spend his time at the shelter with her trying to explain the reasons for her solitude. What if he found the contact information of the woman who took the other one and called her? What if he told her that some of her paperwork was missing or confessed that the dogs needed to at least say goodbye so they didn't crumble under the sadness. He has no idea what it is to sniff and lick a farewell, but he senses that it would be helpful to get them together one last time so they can trace the outline of this departure. Or maybe no ritual would be worthy of this goodbye. He guesses it would be useless to try and convince the woman to adopt both dogs. As he releases Mona in the courtyard again, he understands that if he wants to begin to repair what is breaking in that moment, he will need to spend a few nights on the cold tiles of the floor of her cell with her. Pet her in her solitary vigil to make this sudden absence less abrupt. Mitigate, somehow, this new abandonment.

Kati

Though her flesh seems stiff and fragile, Kati tries to remain on her feet at all costs. She fights against the occasional curves and sudden stops that shake her, as if trying to bend her bones. She pants even more, marking with her drool the paper that covers the floor. As they leave the city along a highway ribboned with trucks and buses (that perhaps rumbles like her former streets), her legs give in at last and she lies down. But she keeps her head high, as if suggesting that she has not resigned herself to anything and has not forgotten. Then she begins to howl sharp proclamations that descend into growls and climb their way back into laments. Rebellious songs one might confuse for sadness. Her voice seems not as much charged with anger as with more questions than she ever formulated during her days in the streets. She lets out longer howls than the ones she uttered during her first days of exile in the shelter, when she polished the cell's echoes with her sobs. But Mona isn't there anymore—Mona, hardened like her by abandonment—to calm her. She can't lie down beside her and bury her muzzle in the fur of her neck, as if to assure her that both are welcome.

The woman looks back at her from time to time in the rearview mirror, wondering if it was a good idea to adopt an adult dog instead of a puppy without any baggage.

"Easy now, girl, calm down. Where I'm taking you is a paradise, you'll see. You're going to love it, so much nicer than that freezing pound. You'll see, my girl. We're almost there."

Kati howls even more. Just like the night when they took Luis, her nose is so dry it has gone dull.

"Easy now, you're going to love the field where you'll get to run and the nice soft bed you'll have all to yourself. That's right. And you'll be able to do whatever you want and you'll make friends with Thief, he'll just adore you, he's such a good boy. You're going to be so happy. Now quiet down, sweet girl. No more crying."

Kati's wails defy the appeals of the woman, who turns the radio off and then on again. Overwhelmed by her inability to explain this move, she wonders again where the dog lived before. She imagines a small apartment in the southern part of Bogotá, that her previous owners couldn't keep her because she got too big, like what happened to a friend of hers at work, who took in a dog from her domestic worker. Or she was lost in a park, because dogs often get lost in Bogotá, everyone knows that. Or had she been stolen and escaped her captors? She hopes that the dog didn't grow up in the streets. It wouldn't be so bad if she had spent a few days sniffing through trash on the sidewalk, but to live from birth on the cracked pavement, in the grime of puddle-filled parks, in the dusty caverns under certain bridges from which she always looks away because she knows people use their shadows as camouflage, well, that would be concerning. What had been shattered for her between that life and this one? The woman is certain she could help the dog find happiness if she knew.

When Kati stops howling, trumpets blast over the radio in a symphony that celebrates distant triumphs. The woman turns up the volume, hoping that this melody will brighten her new companion's dark mood. Panting, Kati seems to ignore the music echoing amid the revving motor, the rattling air conditioner, the rumbling tires. Maybe she's thirsty. The woman can't see her in the rearview mirror but is glad that she stopped crying.

During the two and a half hours of the trip, each time Kati rises to express her displeasure, the woman reminds her in a singsong from the driver's seat that she is beautiful and brave. Though her ears perk up, the dog refuses to look at the source of that voice. She unfurls her body curved and awkward, as if unsure of where to rest her bones, perhaps suspecting danger deep in the fibers of her muscles, still appearing perplexed by her own flesh. She has never seen the earth unfold so quickly.

The tree-flecked fields, the hills sown with corn and potato, the dump trucks and tractor trailers that the car passes on its long way up the mountain. Discolorations on the other side of the fogged glass. But maybe Kati doesn't wonder about any of that. Her eyes seem to want to coil toward an inner trembling. Cloistered in metal, perhaps she can't get a clear scent of the distant dogs and cows, uprooted plants, excrement and insecticide, smoke from brickmakers and bonfires, ploughed fields, chicken feathers. Is there a breath of hope beneath her panting? Disoriented, and maybe even nauseated after all this jostling, perhaps, but a breath of hope that might speak of more than exile.

When the car finally stops after the buffeting of potholes in the unpaved road on the last leg of their journey, Kati pops up, as if launched by a spring. At the edge of the open trunk, while the wind blows through her fur, she observes in a daze fields and forests that don't give off the slightest scent of asphalt or combustion or the disinfectant they used at the pound. Her muzzle reveals her curiosity when she breathes in the affable body of a new woman coming toward her. She probably notices the chicken fat and lanolin that cling to the woman's apron, her hands magnetized by onion, cilantro, and detergent. Behind this other woman's robust flesh, perhaps Kati perceives the fibers and resins of the new foliage on the breeze, and the traces of the myriad animals that cleave those lands. Does she hear an echo of her past? Maybe she wonders about Luis, or Mona, or the man from the pound. Whether one of them is waiting for her nearby. Or maybe none of that.

No one who might see her there, tense and immobile on the threshold of that dirty car, would imagine her boldness. How often she has leaped over walls and wagons. How when she breaks into a gallop she is unconstrained by the weight that now oppresses her.

The woman asks her housekeeper to hold the dog's leash.

"We don't want her running away, after all that. Her name is Lady, but we're going to have to give her a new one."

The housekeeper pets the dog's head, trying to understand her despondency.

"Hello, pretty girl. Congratulations, Miss Gloria, she's beautiful. Look at that shiny fur, and she's not too skinny at all. They took good care of this one."

Resigned, Kati lets this new woman pet her and does not growl; she makes herself small but avoids the searching gaze of both.

"Don't congratulate me, Teresa—you'll be taking care of her too."

"The only thing, Miss Gloria, is maybe it would be best not to change her name yet, since that will just confuse her more and what we want is for her to settle in."

The caretaker lifts the dog and places her on the ground without a moment's hesitation, just as she has always done with calves, chickens, and sheep.

Kati stretches and arches her back when her paws touch the ground, as if trying to lubricate with vigor her joints stiffened by the journey. She seems not to know what to do with her tail, whether to hide it or free it from the prison of her legs. Perhaps the moment her paws come in contact with the grass, something in her tells her to run, to gallop across the fields and mountains in search of Luis. Or does she want to return to Mona? It might also be that displacement has mutilated her desires. Or that, getting her first taste of the forest and its decomposing leaves, of water's persistence in seeping through countless hollows, she finally begins to gauge her loss.

Bound by the leash, she pulls the caretaker to one of the flowerbeds that surround the house and leaves a large puddle of urine beside a worm. The dark, lumpy ground under the hydrangeas must be a very new smell for her. Everything certainly must sound different. A vast expanse without machines. A host of trees greater than any she has seen, which suffocates all sound when they rustle in the breeze. She points her muzzle at the mountaintop then down toward the small hills and plateaus that stretch out in front of her. All that foliage, unbroken by buildings or cars, must seem completely foreign to her. Perhaps she feels that unfamiliarity in her flesh.

In Bogotá, she only crossed once through a forest into the mountains, when she still lived with Luis. She climbed the narrow streets of Barrio Egipto at Luis's side, then passed through eucalyptus trees and pines until they reached an elevated clearing. Who knows if she remembers anything of the chubby, tangled clouds at sunset or the orange cloud of dust hanging like a tarp over that westward-stretching city, the smell of a mountain far removed from that smog, a scent so new to her.

Taking the world in through her nose, letting its resins permeate her holes, smear her viscera, and hum. Sniffing the darkest earth she has ever stood on, smelling the oak grove draped in moss, with its cushion of leaves and its warp and weft of mushrooms, and the persistent spirit of the stream flowing below. Grazing the fog that creeps inside her. Sensing the corpses of all those creatures that hold the soil up and hearing the buzz of all those insects. How does she make sense of all this for the first time? What some would call the unsung, sometimes unpleasant, work of getting new bearings. Others would call this task joyous for the ways it is liberating.

Thief bounds up to greet her, barking the way only a spoiled dog who has never howled over an absence can bark. As if in recognition that she is the newcomer, Kati falls still again and stiffens. Her hackles raise and she growls softly as he eagerly breathes in her anus and vulva. She seems ready to growl at him with all the fury of her days defending their cart in the streets. Thief wags his tail and rolls onto his back beside her, as if offering an apology and inviting her to be his master. She doesn't appear convinced. She smells him again hesitantly, perhaps letting him know that she hasn't yet accepted his promise of friendship. Thief is bigger than she is but seems to understand that, though broken when she arrived, Kati is guided by a sovereign rage. Subdued for the moment, but latent.

Kati pulls the woman who holds her by a leash farther, toward the edge of the garden. Maybe if she were in the street or with Mona at the shelter she wouldn't follow the path, meek, as if asking permission. Thief follows them, shimmying loose and happy, making even more apparent the despair that garrots Kati's flesh. Both women feel relieved that the dogs have not fought.

The afternoon dims, so the frogs can begin making their ruckus. Perhaps Kati is surprised by those diaphanous chants that never echoed downtown (only her distant ancestors, the ones who lived over a century ago, would have heard the frogs in the Vicachá River before all the trees that held it were felled and they hid it under Bogotá's cement, robbing it of its name and its creatures). The woman who adopted her has decided that the dog should spend the night in the house because she is afraid her new companion will run away, even though when she moved there she promised herself she wouldn't sleep with animals inside her home ever again and has trained Thief to stay outside. Kati crosses the threshold reluctantly, gently resisting the tug of the leash. When she realizes that she has been released, she finds herself a nook in the kitchen as fast as a hunting wolf and curls up in the broom corner. Not even when the brooms come crashing down on her does she accept the woman's offer of a place to rest on the carpet under the table or the plate of food she holds out.

"Why so worried, pretty girl? Can't you see you're in your new home? Don't look at me like that, I wouldn't lie to you."

The woman remembers that she decided to address this one more warmly, and for the first time feels uncomfortable talking to a dog.

"I know it's hard to move house, Lady, but your life is going to be just great here, you'll see. So much better than in Bogotá. Yes, that's right, because you're a brave and beautiful girl."

Kati pants and looks at the door, vigilant.

The woman is dismayed that she can't read the animal's thoughts. Could she be questioning her kindness? Does she doubt her reasons for bringing her here? She wonders if the dog will ever show her the gratitude she deserves and thinks again about how jarring her name is, though she knows it would be a terrible idea to change it right now.

Kati dodges the piece of cheese the woman holds out to her and tries to fold even farther into herself, gathering herself toward her ribs when the woman tries to pet her. Eventually, perhaps realizing that she's cornered, Kati allows the woman to rub the top of her head. The woman asks herself again if she made a mistake, if she shouldn't have gotten a dog whose past was known. She regrets not waiting a few more months and buying one of the puppies her friend's Labrador just delivered, though she's asking a fortune for them. Then the niece who convinced her to adopt a homeless dog pops into her mind, and she remembers how admirable it is to relieve another living creature of its solitude. In the first photo she takes, her new companion is curled up, melancholy, staring at a horizon beyond the walls that enclose her. She sends it to her niece, and adds:

Look who came home with me from the shelter!
Her name is Leti. Slowly settling in!

Kati sniffs the freshly mopped tile, which gives off a scent that must be new to her, so different from the wood of her cart, the soot on the street, and the bleach in her cell. She occasionally cranes her neck and looks out the dining room window, as if eager to be outside. Her panting catches between her black lips when she tries to rest her head again. She jumps several times at the loud pop of logs crackling in the fireplace. Though her muzzle is buried against her stomach, she twists her gaze to observe, from the corner of her eye, the woman pacing around, practicing how to be her owner. She watches her unpack boxes and luggage. She seems unsettled by the passion in the woman's voice as she sings boleros. She tracks the woman's comings and goings the way a prisoner might study a guard.

She begins to bark while the woman is in the bathroom, torturing the ingrown toenail that for years has been home to a fungus. She is answering the call of four huge mastiffs, caged in a nearby finca, which howl their despairing melodies every night. In the distance, the dogs seem to be cursing the cosmos for their captivity, as if singing the nostalgic ballad of a roving ancestral past. Thief joins in outside. Kati perks her ears and raises her hackles, perhaps trying to decipher this sad song. The woman hopes her new dog isn't infected by the others' sorrows.

"I know you miss your old life. I do. But don't you go listening to those other dogs complaining over there. They don't live here. And you're free! Look, you can even sleep in my room tonight. Come! Now you'll be able to relax, you'll see. Come on! Lady!"

The woman stomps her feet a little and notices that the dog, without moving, glances at her, as if scrutinizing her bones. She thinks of all the reproaches she would be receiving from her mother, who had raised all her poodles with ironclad discipline and absolutely no fawning, content with the authority that came with forcing them to follow all kinds of orders while she followed those of her husband. If the old woman were still alive, she would be questioning—again—her daughter's softheartedness, her impulse to embrace and be licked by every dog she sees. She also would have criticized the dog's name and her dubious provenance.

Kati lowers her muzzle and lets out one last bark through closed lips. The woman knows it's not a good idea to force her to move from where she is. She wishes she could persuade her to do *something* before the end of the day but doesn't know what else to ask. She worries that the game of entreaties they began that morning might last too long. That the two of them might tire out. She wonders if the shelter would take the dog back.

"All right, you sleep there like a good girl. Don't make a racket, now, because we all need to rest after this long day and all the trouble I went through to bring you here. Tomorrow you'll start to settle in, okay? You will, you'll see. And you'll also learn to show a little gratitude, you hear me?"

Kati locks her eyes on the curtains, as if the woman were a nuisance keeping her from deciphering the whimpers of the other dogs.

After the round of Sudoku she forces herself to complete every night to stave off dementia, the woman inserts a pair of earplugs. She knows she should remain alert in case the dog misbehaves somehow, but she worries that another night of bad sleep could get her migraines going again and kick off a fresh bout of the insomnia she has been suffering for months, ever since her mother died, when she and her seven siblings started eyeballing everything the old woman had left behind, down to the last spoon, calculating what it was worth and how deeply it moved them, and the fights began.

Before burrowing under the covers that protect her from the cold that tends to seep through the pores of her new home, the woman worries that the dog might urinate on a carpet or that she might gnaw or scratch a piece of the furniture she just inherited and had shipped from Bogotá to those mountains, at great effort and expense. Large armoires, tables, and bergères that she couldn't bring herself to sell and which she knows are far too ornate for this small, rustic house. Objects that remind her of her mother's enormous home, the place in which she spent her childhood and on which she had needed to daub so much patience while caring for the old woman. She is tired and knows the dog will not heed her tonight. She forbids herself from assuming that the new arrival will disrupt the nocturnal stillness she has so treasured since she buried her mother. She walks to the doorway, says a quick good night that Kati seems not to hear, turns out the lights, and closes the door halfway.

Kati rises for a drink of water once the woman is asleep and empties the bowl with desperate lapping. She sniffs but does not touch the food. Perhaps displacement has taken her appetite. She wanders around the living room, which is also the dining room; the sofas and the armchair, the curtains and the Persian rug seem to say nothing to her. She smells the fibers and shiny veneers of those objects she has never seen before and has no sense of their purpose or past. She sniffs the edges of the refrigerator, as if searching for signs of the life within. The wind picks up, and the bells that hang on the patio intone a solemn, hollow solitude. Kati perks her ears, as if trying to understand them. Do they remind her of the tinkling of the ice cream cart pushed by the man who always said hello to Luis on Carrera Séptima? She barks at the front door, as if getting ready for another round of howls but instead decides to return to her chosen corner and lie down. Maybe because it itches, or maybe just out of habit, she gnaws at the spot where her back meets her tail, like she has done since she was a puppy. Perhaps it reminds her of Luis, who would dig around in her fur whenever he saw her scratching like that, afraid that she had mange. She sneezes and licks her paws with a loving tongue, as if feeling sorry for herself. What musk of Mona's still clings to her fur? What residue, what strand tangled in with her own coat announces that the other is still there, tells the story of the time they spent curled up together? She coils her body as if she were shattered. Three wails catch in her muzzle, heard by no one.

When she does manage to sleep, her paws occasionally twitch as if she were running. Sometimes she puffs hard through her cheeks but doesn't wake, or a solitary muscle twitches. She must be escaping those people who want to hold her captive, chasing the van that took Luis away, crossing Tercer Milenio park to greet another dog, rolling around with Mona in that brief cosmos she found in the courtyard at the shelter. And what if her dream is not the sediment of memory but rather a prophecy? Trotting across the fields, scrambling under a barbed wire fence to search for food, finding a real den, galloping wherever she wants, to Luis or Mona or the man who took care of her at the shelter. Or maybe she only dreams of smells or pinwheels of color, bright fractals, hurricanes, delicious bone marrow, or incomprehensible things we'll never know.

In the morning, Kati hurries to rise when the woman approaches to pet her. Her joints still move like rusty hinges. She refuses to look at the bowl of food the woman holds out to her.

"How is my pretty girl doing this morning? Yes, what a pretty doggie, what a brave doggie in her new home. Such a good girl."

The woman casts her pleas through lips pursed by tenderness, encouraging her to eat. It must sound strange to Kati, who has never had such wheedling melodies foisted on her before. No one—not Luis, not her friends in the street, not the man at the shelter—ever tried to ply her with cloying, plaintive praise. She watches the woman from her corner with her back arched against the wall, and the woman wonders if those brown eyes are begging for something she can't discern, or if they are cursing her for the change of home. She cuts a piece of meat and leaves it near her.

"You're going to like this for sure. You're a bit stubborn, but I understand. They've always called me fiery, but I think that's a good thing, especially in this world where everyone is so scared all the time, where women talk like little girls and smile to please everyone all the time. That's right, beauty. I like people who say what they feel."

After smelling it for longer than she would have inspected any streetside leftover in Bogotá, Kati swallows the meat. Perhaps it tastes exquisite. Maybe she's never eaten anything so fresh in her entire life.

The woman is happy that the dog has taken a piece of meat, but at the same time is annoyed at her lack of gratitude. She wants to ask if she would rather be in the freezing pound than here, where she was so well taken care of, but she restrains herself. When she opens the curtains, the dog stares at the cloud-draped crags.

"Why don't you go outside, then, and say hello to your friend Thief. He's been waiting for you."

As she watches her new dog cross the threshold, stealthy and hunched, the woman wonders what would happen if she ran away. At Animal Care, they had told her that Lady was microchipped, but she hadn't asked where the chip had been implanted or how it worked. She imagines a device that sends a signal from her chest to an antenna but guesses the waves wouldn't be strong enough to find a lost dog at the top of one of these mountains where the peaks seem endless and it is nearly impossible to get a cell phone signal. If her new companion ran off, it was entirely possible that no one would see her cross the landscape, populated as it was by only a few old farmers who refused to exile themselves to the city and a few country homes owned by urbanites who rarely visit them.

Like someone wary of a trap, Kati walks slowly along the corridor that borders the house, where the geraniums that the woman recently brought from the city have begun to flower. She holds back as Thief leaps toward her like a giant grasshopper, raising her tail without growling and arching her back to stretch beside him. Somewhat reluctantly, as if needing to perform certain rituals mandatory for those of their blood, she sniffs the anus of the other dog—who is on his back with his tail wagging—for a few seconds. Then she ignores him when he flips over with a little hop, begging her to play.

She interrupts her walk toward the garden to rest her muzzle on one of the moribund beetles with their backs on the tiles, kicking the air after a night of trying to turn over. Maybe the smell of turmoil emanating from the unfamiliar insect in its agony is new to her. Determined, she heads for the plants with a more assured gait, similar to the one she had when she would trot ahead of Luis on Avenida Jiménez, searching for bones on the sidewalk. She urinates between the hydrangeas and the cala lilies and shits beside a lily of the Nile. She stands for a while with her face to a breeze that wafts a scent of silt from the stream, probably one of the lightest and sweetest to ever make its way inside her. Perhaps the dew suggests something of her cold mornings in the park with Luis just before he was taken. But there is no question that, in these forest-clad mountains at the foot of peaks that hold the highest plains, the wind spreads a different film across her viscera. How does she sound the depths of the landscape stretched before her? The huge trees swaying patiently, asserting their intent to remain, the cliffs murmuring the centuries, the mushrooms that multiply along subterranean currents, the hawk circling above and the swallows' faithful pilgrimage. Maybe it is that effervescence of limbs, sludge, and foliage that makes her tuck her tail and turn her muzzle skyward, to pore over all that fertility and putrefaction, all those remnants. Does it ease her suffering a bit?

The buzz of a nearby bee unsettles her. She pricks her ears and tries to focus her eyes on the enigma masturbating a flower. Kati studies this stranger, perhaps trying to understand how it could be that she isn't a fly. She has no way of knowing that the bee is a foreigner to those parts too, that three months earlier a van hired by the woman displaced her entire hive from the kingdom they had always inhabited and deposited them in these rainy mountains, right after the queen bee had gone into exile and the new queen had begun laying eggs to repopulate the clan. Most of them died on that journey, crushed or drowned in honey. Those who survived emerged into a bewildering world of downpours and fog to forge new routes to flowers they had never seen before. Kati doesn't know that the bee has also endured an ambush and has spent months searching for and memorizing new paths—just as she must now do—or that, despite the residues of her harrowing journey, she continues to spit, generous, the treacle of her innards.

The woman takes advantage of the fact that the day is brightening and the clouds aren't as meddlesome as usual to ask her housekeeper to bathe the dog when she comes to do her morning chores. The woman knows, because the cousin who sold her the house told her, that the neighbor she hired has a way with animals; some say she can even tell the future by the sound of their buzzing, howls, songs, and bleats. In the newcomer's first interview with the woman, who had lived there her entire life, the latter had explained how she could speak with many beings, understand their sorrows and sense their secret rhythms. That she could save cows with their calves stuck inside without losing the birth, raise orphaned calves and foals, tell which bleats indicate sickness and which suggest a retained placenta. That she could help cows and horses suffering with bloat from eating damp grass after a frost, treat convulsive dogs with massage, revive the poisoned ones, and cure any living thing stung by a scorpion or stuck by a porcupine, even humans. From the window, the woman peers at her housekeeper as she pats the dog gently on the haunch, scrubs her wet fur, and uncoils the tail she has tucked between her legs without the dog protesting. The newcomer dislikes how the other woman sings rancheras off-key but is glad to have hired her, even though some days it feels indulgent to dedicate part of her pension to the housekeeper's salary.

Kati takes a few small steps to avoid the hose, but the housekeeper traps her between her unerring knees. Scented shampoo cuts a path through her coat before falling to the patio tiles, carrying away the last traces of Mona with the foam. With what vestige will Kati remember her former companion now?

"This water's colder than ice, I know it, but we're almost done and won't you be elegant. They never gave you a bath in that pound, did they? Just coming from the city you've got to be full of muck. I know you hate it, but you'll feel better after, you'll see. A fresh start."

Maybe Kati remembers the bath they gave her the day she arrived at the shelter, the first time she'd ever been hosed down. The sickly-sweet smell of the soap and the acrid powder they dusted her with at the end, which she tried in vain to rub off against the dirty walls of her cell. And how her skin twitched until the man took her out to the courtyard to warm herself on the sunbaked cement.

"Easy now, don't you go worrying that we'll be bothering you all the time. No, ma'am. Unless you get it in your head to start swimming in those swampy puddles down there like Thief, he comes back a sight and gets mud all over everything, then there's nothing to it but the hose."

Kati looks away from her, as if offended, and waits stoically until the woman has finished drying her with a towel before shaking herself off.

"And don't you go forgetting that this is your home now. You hear me, Lady?"

She shivers as if not only from the humid cold but also the starkest abandonment. Thief dances his way up to her, but she dodges him and runs to the garden to tangle herself in the shrubs and roll around in the grass.

From inside, the other woman flings the window open too forcefully.

"Dammit, Teresa, won't she just run away?"

"Don't you go worrying, Miss Gloria. She's a little fired up still, but it'll pass. You can be sure of it because I explained how this is where she lives now, and she understood so she'll stay."

Kati spends the first few days rooted to the ground, as if a subterranean force were trying to suck her down to the center of Earth. When they ripped Luis from her months earlier, she had searched for traces of him all over the cracked streets of Bogotá she had known since she was a puppy. When they deported her to Animal Care, she had called to him for days with growls and saliva-flecked rage until she finally accepted Mona's invitation to tussle. Maybe her rootlessness in these mountains of deep roots and utterly new creatures has shredded her maps, scrambled her compass. Or could it be that all those relocations wore down her fury? It might be that Kati is unsure what appetites to cultivate among the flutter of that foliage. Perhaps this frustrates or exhausts her. Or maybe she senses that she can better decipher the buzz of the creatures gamboling around her if she remains perfectly still. She sleeps little, though she spends long hours lying down. Folded into her own flesh as if trying to disappear, she occasionally raises her head to investigate the dance of trees clinging to their mud. Impossible to know what their scents return to her. Sometimes, with her head on the ground, she watches the women from the corner of her eye as they come and go around the house. Her ears perk up whenever their conversation echoes her way, or when the neighbor sings while organizing another woman's home.

Kati doesn't seem to mind when the clouds arrive, calm and clinging, to shroud the peak those women try to convince her is hers and settle into her mane without conquest. After so many late nights on the streets of Bogotá, perhaps Kati likes that the moist veil of that fog returns a bit of shine to her nose, which has been so dry lately.

As time passes, she seems more gracious toward Thief, who continues to beg her for romps she is not ready to offer. She no longer raises her hackles when he approaches. Sometimes, in solidarity, she even barks with him when the squeal of a dog or a motorcycle echoes through the highlands. After her first few days, she begins to accompany him every morning when he heads down to the front gate to greet the neighbor as she arrives to clean. While the other jumps and whines, she wiggles her rib cage and circles the woman a couple of times. Along the alder-lined path that leads to the house, she synchronizes her trot to the woman's gait.

Sometimes, when she rises from the corner of the patio where she spends her hours of bewilderment, she makes the pilgrimage to the garden that borders the property's field, where she studies bumblebees and grasshoppers that didn't exist on her streets. She dedicates long lapses to smelling the black dirt that holds water like treasure, perhaps trying to understand the story of countless viscera rotting away, the mingling of urine and excrement, the bones and exoskeletons that narrate lives and their endings from every heap of soil. From there, she scrutinizes the mountains when the clouds allow. Sometimes her ears prick up. It seems she is still gathering the strength she needs to cross the bushes and venture toward the forest where old and new bees trace their routes, along with so many other beings that climb and buzz, all still so strange to her.

Every so often, the woman will spy on her through the dining room window, distracting herself from the pain of unpacking objects inherited from her mother, a task she has been putting off for months but has finally found the energy to address with the arrival of the new dog. She pulls her mother's belongings from the boxes without any idea whether to keep them or give them away, to whom or where or why. She is particularly flummoxed by a small crystal box in which her mother had stored fifteen teeth—some milk teeth, and others with roots—that she'd lost at different moments in her life. It soothes her to turn from time to time and watch the dog, wilted on the patio tiles, ruminating over her luggageless wanderings. Spying on the dog helps her understand that she is not obligated to cherish what her mother loved, and that there is a vast difference between inheriting the timeworn possessions of another and inheriting their love for those possessions. On the second day she has the dog in her care, she buries the collection of teeth in the garden, quietly grateful to her new companion.

Perhaps Kati does not feel the woman's eyes on her in the garden where the moribund seedlings relocated from Bogotá decide whether or not this is a worthy place to grow. She growls whenever she feels the woman approach her from behind, promising caresses. Perhaps that anxious voice begging her to accept the offered comfort carries a disquieting odor. Who knows whether in some deep crevice inside her, Kati remembers other ambushes when the woman draws near. Like when she was still living with Luis and she approached the cart of a recycler who hated him and received a blow with a stick that left her limping for days. Or when they trapped her on the rubble of the street she and Luis once called home.

Each time Kati grumbles, the woman takes it as a defeat. She fantasizes about calling the famous trainer she has seen on that television series, who can make himself the master of any pet and crush the rebellion of any animal who fails to understand their place in the household. It bothers her not to have a clear sense of why her dog is not adjusting. She oscillates between congratulating herself for rescuing the animal from the loneliness of Bogotá and blaming herself for bringing her to an unfamiliar place. She doesn't know how else to make her new companion feel welcome, aside from showering her with more praise, which she suspects would be rejected. The woman's neighbor has suggested patience, and the woman tries to convince herself that the dog will gradually get used to the mountain. She hopes the pieces of meat that are now accepted without hesitation have begun to bridge the distance quivering between them. She clings to her small victories and keeps score. The dog finishes her meal with enthusiasm. The dog allows her ears to be scratched after eating. The dog accepts praise without withdrawing. The dog doesn't growl when she sinks her hand into the fur on her neck. The dog looks at her when called, even if just briefly and even if she refuses to come when beckoned. The dog walks with her head higher and tenses her mane less often. The woman promises herself time and again that they will eventually love one another as they should, and that the orphanhood still seeming to fester in her new companion will gradually dissipate. That she will soon abandon her ungrateful ways and wake up as confident as she'd been in the shelter when the woman first saw her, glad to accept her caresses. That when she does, she will be able to go on walks with Thief, happy at their side on the old foot trails the woman has gradually been discovering in the area. The woman has wondered more than once what she will do otherwise.

Kati spends her first few nights indoors. Since she doesn't seem to want to enter the house at sundown and the woman is wary of antagonizing her, the housekeeper returns every evening to help her get the dog into the kitchen. Kati meekly lets the neighbor lead her, docile and defeated, to the corner she chose on her first day, where now there is a soft mat made of blankets taken from a box of inherited objects. It might be a combination of rage and worry that gathers in her eyes as she collapses onto the pile. She watches the woman surreptitiously while she eats, tidies the kitchen, pours herself a glass of whiskey, turns on the news. Quick movements of her ears track strange noises from the television and sharp notes in the woman's voice when she speaks on the phone. She raises her head when the woman begins to sing boleros and tangos the way Luis used to sing vallenatos. Sometimes she sits up, as if unsettled by the stillness, but she lies down again before long. When she senses the woman looking at her, she turns her eyes to meet hers, briefly, as if annoyed. From time to time, she tenderly licks her paws.

She stands and barks each time the dogs imprisoned on the neighboring property intone their nocturnal elegy. Perhaps she feels sympathy for them. There might be resignation behind the way she allows herself to be pet after she barks with them, looking the other way as the woman's fingers tangle in the fur on her neck in an attempt to calm her. Perhaps she is beginning to accept the role of satisfying the woman's eagerness to protect her (to protect herself?), which is the fate of so many dogs.

In the middle of her third night, Kati barks at the dining room window with nearly the same intensity as when she would defend their cart from strangers in Bogotá. Did she smell one of the opossums that make their rounds through the garden? Is she curious about the beetles that slam constantly into the glass? Or is she, perhaps, expelling a rage she has been harboring for a long time, the fury Mona seemed to soothe? Kati ignores the woman's invitation to lie down again, even when a piece of meat is involved. She barks a little longer. Thief answers her from outside. Despite the pills she took, the woman lies awake wondering what to do if the dog continues disturbing her sleep.

On the fourth night, Kati enters the house when called, docile, without anyone needing to force her. The woman tells herself it was not a mistake to adopt her and sends her girlfriends in the group chat a photo she took of the dog in the garden, among the lilies of the Nile. Kati is standing in profile with her ears pricked, staring into the cloud forest.

This is Leti, my new companion.

She has always hated it when people call themselves their dog's mother or father. She receives confetti, hearts, and happy emoticons, then sends her thanks in reply. She forwards the same photo to her three favorite nieces, her coworker at the bank who hasn't retired yet, and the housekeeper who cleaned her apartment in Bogotá for fifteen years and helped her raise Thief. She likes the praise. She likes that they think the dog is as beautiful as she does, and that they all know she organized her rescue. The goodness that swells her chest also makes her happy.

When the house is dark, Kati sets her front paws on the kitchen counter and steals a chicken that the woman has left there to thaw. She spends the small hours caressing its juices and scratching at the fibers of its hardened breast. Each time she runs her tongue over the bird seems to bring her happiness, as if for the first time since the love of Mona and the others was ripped from her, this mission were beginning to weave tissue over the gaping wound of her pain. Extracting time in the form of flavors and appetizing juices. Participating in the transmutation of another's flesh.

The next night, the dog scratches insistently at the door that the woman just had installed, leaving a signature of deep grooves in the wood. It seems that in the dark she is recovering the lost vigor of her claws, the lightning that flashes across the mounds of her gumline, the troubadour power of her deep voice. Perhaps after heartbreak she has rediscovered the strength to delight in unsullied morning air, avian hullaballoo, the scent of industrious mice, for all that crackles and crystallizes when day is trying to break.

At sundown on the sixth day, no one forces Kati inside.

The woman moves Kati's bed out to the covered area where Thief sleeps and leaves a piece of fresh meat on it that the dog immediately inhales.

"Are you happy to be sleeping outside now?"

Kati examines the blankets, which give off a synthetic odor, then looks away, as if rejecting them, trying to detect movement in the forest. Perhaps, after a lifetime of the diurnal songs of sparrows and thrushes and the nocturnal silence of urban birds, she is surprised to hear the ululation of an owl in a nearby tree. Darkness transformed into the cry of a bird of prey.

"But don't you even think about going to look for those dogs they have locked up over there or exploring the forest at night. I'll take you out there soon, just as soon as you're ready to join us on our walks. It won't be long, I'm sure. But for now you get some rest out here with Thief and keep an eye on the house together, all right?"

The woman crouches and tries to pet the dog, wanting to cup her muzzle in her hands the way she always does with the other one. She wants to kiss the dark fur shining on the animal's head, but she restrains herself. For the first time she is able to see, up close, the brown border that adorns her pupils like the rocky crater of a flooded volcano. Thief wedges himself between them, always eager to be pet, and the woman kisses him on the forehead after wiping away the sticky saliva he deposited on her.

"You take good care of her."

The woman wonders how long it will be before her new dog's evasive eyes search for hers. Whether the day will arrive when her gaze is transformed into an entreaty, a request for affection, the way Thief looks at her, when she will at least drop the shield of mistrust she has raised between herself and all she observes since she arrived.

Instead of lying down beside Thief, Kati heads for the patio, accepting on her way another piece of meat thrown at her by the woman, who follows her. Kati lets the woman pat her on the haunches a few times and scratch the hair behind her ears, where perhaps she holds another memory of Luis, who would dig around back there until she fell asleep. Is she beginning to sense that she has no choice but to submit to this courtship and extortion? It might also be that, after years of begging for bones, the juicy chicken thigh has begun to splinter the rebellion that resides in her. When she lies down on the patio rug, she allows herself to be covered with another blanket, which gives off a strange perfume that must render the absence of her old companions even more acute.

During the hours when Kati rests on the patio before making her escape, the woman watches a news report about the discovery of more mass graves in Antioquia that are believed to contain the victims of paramilitary groups. One shot shows a forest clearing roped off and guarded by two police officers and a German shepherd. She hears the ruckus of the birds competing with the voice of the forensic investigator as he stands beside a grave that had contained fourteen corpses and explains the details of their findings. She wonders if it had only been that one dog helping to detect the bodies hidden under so many layers of earth. It angers her that no one mentions him, and she promises herself that she'll send an email to the program first thing in the morning. In a few months, she thinks, when everything feels less tenuous and she stops wondering if it was really a good idea to rent out her apartment in Bogotá and come live on this mountain, she could consider adopting another dog. When her friends finally come visit her and the vegetable garden is growing well and she has unpacked all her boxes. When the new dog has finally understood that this is her home. Hopefully one of those canine heroes. But if not, another from the shelter. In one segment of the program, a blonde in a red cocktail dress reads advertisements for cell phone plans before introducing a special called "Do You Have a Dog? They'll Love You for Doing These Five Things." For a moment, the woman gets her hopes up, thinking it might give her the tip she needs to finally win over her new companion. Instead, a muscular dog trainer in a track suit makes trite observations while walking a Labrador through a park in northern Bogotá. The woman turns the television off with disdain, pours herself another whiskey, and peeks outside to make sure Kati is still there.

Kati joins the distant wails of the fenced-in dogs with her own barks of solidarity for a while after the woman turns out the lights, and ignores her when she pops her head out, as if wanting to be alone in what she is doing. She does not seem relieved by the congratulations the woman tosses at her for staying or by her promises that she'll sleep well right where she is.

The dog gets up as soon as the lights in the house go out again. She stretches and shakes herself off, as if shedding the docility she has needed to feign. With her nose she embraces the air, aiming her muzzle at the stream she visited with Thief and the woman that morning, where she smelled for the first time those waters that lap at the iron in the rocks and plough through sediment. How many animals and fetid odors arrive from afar at that hour to tickle her senses? Perhaps she detects from there the paths cut by rodents through the moss and tree trunks. The buzzing of beetles addicted to light. The weightless discipline of spiders and the frenzy of moths. The drool and death of so many creatures.

On the path that leads to the front gate she begins to trot, eager, with her muzzle close to the ground, just like she used to do in Bogotá, in the early hours when she would wake before Luis and search for rats in the park. She slips under the wooden gate that the housekeeper secures with a padlock each afternoon and sets out on the unpaved road where several motorcycles and the milk truck pass by every day, but which is completely empty at this hour. A new joy seems to shake her bones. Urgency appears to have taken her over.

She stops whenever something catches her attention from the side of the road, leaping excitedly to sniff out whatever is trying to hide in the jumble of leaves, as if those detours might unearth substances to alleviate a long-held affliction. Then she returns to the dirt road that takes her south, perhaps remembering her destination and purpose. Her light gait and loose tail reveal her newfound ease.

Loping unchecked toward the trees that border the road, urinating on whatever stick she chooses, poking her muzzle in musky hollows. Detecting in an instant the resins other beings smear across the ground. Hearing the call of so much flesh begging to be tracked. Sniffing at length other pilgrimages and excrements, the oily scaled life of skin and substance that blankets the world. Exhaling, as if overstuffed, when she comes across the trace of a new body. What do the feathers of the birds asleep above her smell like? The rubbery skin of frogs expanding in the stream? Rat urine? Worm trails across a rock? The tiny flecks that fall from the wing of a moth? Invading the mossy sponge that soaks her paws. Chewing herbs that don't taste like sooty grass. Rubbing herself against the rotting corpse of some rodent to leave her coat well perfumed. Walking smug and satisfied like she used to do along the edge of Carrera Décima, though everything smells and sounds different, though she no longer noses every discarded scrap hungrily. Going wherever she wants without the magnet of Luis pulling her toward a return. Exploring as if there were no such thing as thresholds. Anyone who saw her would say she is finally setting out on her own, obeying her own will.

Maybe Kati senses that someone is waiting for her, since she turns confidently onto the narrow path that winds its way to the other woman's house, tucked into the base of the next hill. She spends a moment examining the cows sleeping in a nearby field, never having seen them up close. She growls. Do they remind her at all of the carved bodies hanging in the butcher shops downtown, or is the living animal's scent very different? A light shines beside the little house, and she heads toward it. A cat climbs deftly onto the roof. Kati explores her surroundings calmly, sniffing the cracks in the laundry room floor, the uchuva and blackberry bushes in the dark vegetable garden. She approaches the pen, where the heavy roundness of a sheep fragrant with lanolin and grass seems to surprise her. She growls again but does not bark. After sniffing the perimeter of the house and the chicken coop, as if finally satisfied with the maps she has sketched, she nuzzles the crack between the door and its frame. There is no question that she recognizes, on the other side of that wood, the woman who greets her every morning with terse tenderness as she passes through the gate of the other house. Kati lies down on the doormat as if it were the den that had been waiting for her all this time. She licks her paws with care and scratches the pads of one with her teeth, perhaps where a splinter worked its way in.

 She flits in and out of sleep. Maybe she is still startled by the song of the owls, which is even louder in that forest that rises nearby. One might even think that after tonight's victory the first layer of her distress has begun to melt away.

María Ospina

Every night over the following weeks, ignoring the entreaties of both women, Kati refuses to sleep beside Thief. On the first few evenings after the start of her wanderings, she goes when ordered to the blankets left for her on the patio by the woman who brought her from Bogotá. She waits for all the lights in the house to go out, gives herself a shake, and frees the joyous springs of her muscles to trot off to the other woman's house. She inspects her surroundings with less zeal than she did at first. Sometimes she lopes along the main road carved by backhoes a decade earlier; other times, she takes the winding path that people have used for hundreds of years, though now only as a shortcut. Sometimes, she forges her own way through the mountainside, skirting ferns, chusque, and lianas. She mines the earth with her nose, then exhales its particles into the air. Perhaps she still discovers traces of new animals that surprise her. Every so often, she stops to contemplate with devotion the universe suggested by a hollow or the edge of a rock. She seems to be honing a new sovereignty. Maybe in the darkness that inspires her to wind through the forest, she is beginning to inhabit another time-place. Not the night of the women's exhausted sleep or Luis's officious watchfulness or the grueling shifts of the women who work in the motels around her park downtown or the hours that seep in through the fluorescent lights in the shelter where Mona still lives under the care of the man who loves them. A welcoming lapse of strides and silt and squawks and trills and smells and fibers and flow impossible to quantify. An echoing, acoustic miasma that shatters duration and all its units of measure.

Only when she is ready, perhaps once the mountain has spoken volumes in spirit and substance; only then does Kati make her way to the caretaker's doorway. Like someone finding a nook for a brief rest after a long ramble.

Every morning, Kati rolls around in front of the woman's modest home when she opens the door, as if thanking her for her hospitality. She romps against the woman's solid legs just like she and Mona would do when the man from the shelter would open the door to their cage. Is she invoking the dance of her friend, who once leaped alongside her? Perhaps with those movements she is expressing her gratitude for the restrained tenderness the woman offers. Maybe she prefers not to have words put to each of her actions, not to have someone always trying to decipher them. It might be that something about the caretaker who invites her into her dark kitchen reminds her of Luis, of how they could be together in silence, of the way he always offered her a frugal, placid friendship, a friendship that respected her peregrinations and never tried to break her spirit. Kati seems to enjoy accompanying the woman as she eats her breakfast beside the woodstove to the rhythm of the music on the radio (the dog happily accepts the bone offered to her), puts the sheep out to pasture, lets the chickens loose, brings the cow water and sprays the saplings that her employer gave her to adorn her home. After that, Kati follows the caretaker along the sinuous route that adapts to the shapes of the mountain until they reach the house where she was supposed to live, and she eats the food offered to her with newfound appetite. She lets the woman who took her from Bogotá pet her, and her bones no longer seem eager to pull away, just as they got used to the man from the shelter.

When Kati first runs away, the woman is beset by a feeling of disappointment not unlike the sensation that washes over her when she gathers rocks that shimmer brilliantly beneath the river's surface but grow pale and dull in the air, refusing to transmit their beauty. She wonders what sneaky ploy her housekeeper has come up with to make the dog want to spend nights with her. She wishes she could rid herself of the jealousy that makes her resent the other woman, who has explained to her that dogs and cats have always sought shelter with her, ever since she was a little girl, because they know she will always open her door to them. Teresa had added that when the dog given to her by a neighbor some ten years earlier died, she had a feeling that someone else would come to keep her company, though she never imagined it would be Lady.

"Miss Gloria, I swear on Mary and all the saints I didn't do anything to make her come to my house."

Her employer hates the pride in her voice but tries not to show it.

"Don't worry on my account, Teresita. I'm getting used to the idea that Leti is an independent creature. Stubborn as a mule is more like it, and does whatever the heck she pleases, but we love her. At least I think she understands now that her life is here. So it's fine if she doesn't sleep at the main house, I don't think she's going to run away, do you? She can have her two houses—she knows we love her, and that's what matters."

Though sometimes she wonders what else she might do to make the dog understand who her real owner is (she even considers tying her up at night but refrains after talking it over with her niece), the woman gradually acknowledges that the animal has a brighter, lighter spirit since she began sleeping outside. So, little by little, she stops poking her head out at night and asking her to stay. She stops getting flustered when the dog spends entire Sundays at the caretaker's house, waiting for her while she goes into town. Not speculating about the dog's activities, not begging her to settle down, fills her with a sense of peace entirely new to her. Understanding that the dog never asked to be hers and that she will never be able to convince her otherwise soothes her initial distress over not being her sole refuge. She is awestruck by the animal's determination after so much displacement. The conviction and courage she trots out on those paths. Sometimes, though she knows it impossible, the woman wishes she could be more like her new companion. Less attached to things. Free of that specifically human way of feeling pain. With a different understanding of abandonment.

In early April, after three months of nocturnal comings and goings between her two homes, when Kati has explored the hills and better understands the motley forest, flocks of migratory birds begin to stir the night air above her. Perhaps she senses the commotion. Does the world smell different when thousands of birds are fluttering toward new lands, botanical dust drifting from their wings? Who knows if Kati notices them and is surprised.

One Sunday morning, while Kati is waiting on the caretaker's doorstep for her to return from town, as has become her habit on the woman's day off, she is startled by the sound of men's voices at the base of the mountain between the two homes. She knows those slopes well; she often makes her way there at night to chase mice, weasels, and squirrels. She has never seen a person among those trees, which might be why she is so surprised to hear shouts coming from beside the stream. A cloud has just arrived to sacrifice itself on the branches, all surrender and satisfaction. Kati probably can't see well through the curtain of fog, but perhaps she catches the scent of the men's sweat as they plot down below.

Kati doesn't know—though the caretaker, who grew up here and has never left, does—that there in the rocky ground held by the forest's roots is an ancient Indigenous burial site. The caretaker's mother, grandmother, and great-grandmother told her of the tunjo that appeared to them on occasion, announcing the graves. A small gold statue of a man glittering in the water, to which they never got too close in case it brought bad luck. The woman remembers how, when she was a little girl, several neighbors found clay pots while tilling the soil. She knows that tomb raiders have long snuck into the unrazed forests nearby to plunder these tree-guarded graves in search of the earthenware, carved figurines, emeralds, and gold buried with people who lived there centuries ago. She has never forgotten her great-grandmother's instruction to always protect the mountain from intruders who seek to disturb the dead, or her grandmother's worry that the looters would be followed by others with plans to cut down their forest. When she was little, around the time her mother ran some men off with her shotgun, she would explore those moss-covered rocks with her brothers, battling mosquitoes, speculating about the lives lodged underground, dreaming about the day she would find an emerald and make them rich. She once found a shard of pottery with red stripes on it inside a rock that had been shattered with dynamite, but she never told anyone. (She still keeps the shard in a kitchen drawer.) Neither her mother nor her grandmother had known what to say when she asked if the bodies in those graves were from the same Indigenous group as the people who, when the Spanish came to persecute them, had jumped off that famous cliff nearby. She never asked herself whether those bones might belong to her own ancestors, though she has never imagined her family coming from anywhere other than this land.

Perhaps from time to time, as she crossed that rocky slope, Kati detected the porous, worn bones that once held people and are now home to fungi and scorpions. Perhaps she can distinguish between their stench and that of the other creatures populating this underground world.

Furious, Kati barks and growls from the field at the men whose shouts echo through the forest. Thief's distant reply seems to add force to her condemnation. With her hackles raised, she might be trying to understand the limits of her realm. In Bogotá, she several times surprised thieves trying to steal from their cart and managed to teach them a lesson. Now, fur standing on end, she gallops toward the grave robbers, who still shout at one another until she is stopped in her tracks by an explosive that resounds among the trees and rebounds against the cliffs. Does she remember how the blasts during the protests downtown frightened her? She would run around like she had lost her mind, scurrying for shelter; later, Luis would find her trembling under the cart. This time, however, she doesn't flee. She bursts into even more furious barking as soon as the echo dissipates and the voices return. The foamy, guttural rage thundering between her teeth resembles her fury the day they took him, when all promises began to break.

Who knows whether the dog notices, absorbed as she is in the men's invasion, the birds scattered from the trees by the blast.

acorn woodpeckers
Andean guans
a screech-owl
carriquí jays
hummingbirds
flycatchers
troupials
warblers
grosbeaks
brushfinches
vireos
a southern emerald-toucanet
and the tanager

Some of them, the ones getting ready to spend many nights flying toward northern summers, are familiar with explosions of that kind; people everywhere find reasons to ignite gunpowder. But even they are startled. Perhaps Kati senses the furtive flutter that lifts them away.

She probably does not catch sight of the scarlet tanager as he flies above her, flustered, expelled too soon from the highest branches of the oak where he had settled for a bit. He had spent restless days gorging himself on insects and seeds, accommodating a new layer of fat in his chest, shedding old feathers to make room for new red ones, preparing for the long journey to the northern forest. He still has a few days of bulking up ahead of him before the astral and magnetic signal to which he is attuned sends him across the continent once more.

Dog and bird coincide, perhaps without realizing it, in their presence in the old-growth forest and in the vibrations of their hearts, which beat frantically after the explosion. In the terror that lingers after living through so many ambushes. And in the nerves they've honed to survive them.

Seeming to overcome her confusion, Kati barks again, sending her spittle through the shadows. She gallops toward the stream at the base of the mountain, where centuries-old arrayán trees twist in fog mingled with smoke. Ignoring her, four men carrying heavy bags run in the opposite direction, away from a great swarm of bees. They are the newcomers the woman brought to the mountain from the outskirts of Bogotá. Perhaps they have gone after the men because they are fed up with trickery.

As if something were holding her back, Kati seems unsure whether she should chase the men. Until one of the bees rams its stinger into her muzzle and others get tangled in her fur, plunging their indignation into her back. The dog shakes herself from head to toe, as if trying to rid herself of the fire that blooms from each puncture. But her anger at the escaping intruders must be stronger, and she gallops after them, pausing a few times to attend to the itching heat before she reaches the men just as they are climbing onto two motorcycles parked on the side of the road. Maybe she thinks, as perhaps she did back in Bogotá, that her legs are as powerful as any machine, that her speed and her bark will prevail. Nearing the back tire of one motorcycle, she lunges at the driver's leg and pulls it with such force that his bike skids in the dirt. Kati leaps forward to bite the other leg, but a swift kick sends her into the ditch. Her ribs slam against a rock. Perhaps she is pierced by an intense cramp. While she recovers from the impact and leaps back onto the road to continue her attack, the men accelerate and win the race. Apparently spent, Kati finally comes to a halt in the cloud of dust and folds herself in two, trying to attend to the stings that likely have begun to burn more intensely. Who knows if the scrapes on her belly and back speak to her of an injustice.

Kati's muzzle will swell from the stings, and she will scratch at the hives on her paws and back for nearly a week. She will occasionally lick the scars left by the rock, and the limp she got from the man's kick will last four days, though she will not give up her nocturnal wanderings. Maybe her bruised ribs squeal at her. Unaware it was grave robbers who assaulted Kati that morning, the women will tend to her with creams and poultices, each in her own way. One will wonder if the dog had tried to escape, if someone had tried to steal her, or if she went looking for a fight. The other will conclude that Kati disturbed the hive while hunting some other creature and got injured while running from the bees.

Many of the exiled birds will return to the hillside where the invasion occurred because they know not to give up a dwelling so easily.

Before beginning the journey to his other lands, the scarlet tanager will spend a few more days on a nearby mountain carpeted for centuries with hospitable trees always willing to be occupied and nibbled, to host the desires of other creatures. There, he will eat ravenously until the fourth night, when the light orders his departure, perhaps to the relief of his nomadic viscera.

The next Sunday morning, Kati will accompany the caretaker to the house of the woman, who has decided that her dog should not be alone while her housekeeper spends her day off in town. But, as soon as she can, Kati will slip from the woman's patio to the doorstep of the other house, near the mountain with the tombs and the bees, where she waits and reigns. Where itinerant birds live from time to time, and others remain.

Perhaps the looting will spark Kati's desire to defend this forest of ancient bones that promises to reveal more and more the miasmas of the dead. Maybe thanks to the invasion, new bonds will bloom in her. Or maybe not. Who knows whether, as she trots satisfied along those paths, she thinks of Mona. If longing still thrums in her, softer every day.

VI

Everywhere

In one place and another, that is, here, there, and everywhere. *acsieque.* To turn one language into another, to translate. *yquy zegucasuca l. yszeguscasuca*

—Anonymous,
Concise Grammar of the Mosca Language (c. 1612)

Felipa says crickets make noise all the time, not even stopping to breathe, so we can't hear the howls of souls in purgatory. The day there are no crickets left, the world will fill with the howls of those souls and we'll all set out running in terror.

—Juan Rulfo, "Macario"

The word, then, must examine the world. The song of the black ducks that swim in highland ponds where melted snow pools echoes in the rocky depths, sinks into them; it drags itself across the punas, makes the flowers on the hard herbs hidden beneath the ichu dance, does it not? . . . The word is more precise, which is why it can confuse. The highland duck's song lets us understand the spirit of the world.

—José María Arguedas,
The Fox from Above and the Fox from Below

First, because it is true, and secondly because the rules of this story—already weighted down with vines, fallen leaves of all types, vegetal curlicues and pansies—demand it, I will say that the river wasn't far.

—Severo Sarduy, *Hummingbird*

ziiiiiiiir   ziiiiiir   ziiiiiir   ziiiiiir   ziiiiiir

tiiturutiiiiit tiiiturutiiiiit

tiit tiiit tiiiit tiiit   tiit tiiit tiiiit tiiit

tuutuutituutiiiiiiiiiiiii   tuutuutituutiiiiiiiiiiiii   tuutuutituutiiiiiiiiiiiii

jjjjjjjjjjjjjjjjjjjjjjjjjjjjjjjjjjjjjjjjjjjjjjjjjjjjjjjjjjjjjjjjjjjjj

tutitutrrriiiiiiiiiiiii   tutitu

ffffffff ffffffffffffff ff ffff fff   ffffff f ffff ffffffffffffffffff ff ffffffff ffff ff

tutui- tutui- tutui   tutui- tutui- tutui

tuti tutiii tutitutiiii

kiukiu-kiukiu kiukiu-kiukiu kiukiu-kiukiu   kiukiu-kiukiu kiukiu-kiukiu kiukiu-kiukiu

rrurru- rrurru rrurru-rrurru   rrurru-rrurru   rrurru-rrurru

cómo quisieeeera ay que tú viveeeeras que tus ojitos jamás se hubieran cerrado nunca y estar miráaaandolos

trrrrrrrrrrrrrrrrrrrrrrrrrrrrrrrrrrrrrrrrrrrrrrrrr   trrrrrr

tuutuutituutiiiiiiiiiiiii   tuutuutituutiiiiiiiiiiiii   tuutuutituutiiiiiiiiiiiii

gzzzzzzzzzzzzzzzzzzz

cómo quisieeeera ay Lady!! Breakfast! Come get it! Don't you go looking for trouble out in those woods!

booouf booooooouf boooooooouf grrrrrrrr   booouf   booooooouuf

About the Author

María Ospina was born in Bogotá, Colombia. She's a professor of Latin American culture at Wesleyan University. Her first book of fiction, the short story collection *Azares del cuerpo*, was published in Colombia, Chile, and Spain, and was translated into Italian and English (*Variations on the Body*). Her stories have appeared in Colombian anthologies and in literary magazines in the United States. She has also written extensively about contemporary Colombian culture in light of legacies of extractivism, violence, and war, including the book *Memory's Conundrum: Literature, Film, and Testimony at the Beginning of the 21st Century*. *Only a Little While Here*, winner of the Colombian National Novel Award (2024) and the Sor Juana Inés de la Cruz Prize for Literature (2023), is her first novel.

About the Translator

Heather Cleary is based in New York and Mexico City. She is the author of *The Translator's Visibility: Scenes from Contemporary Latin American Fiction* and has written about translation for publications such as *LitHub*, *Two Lines*, and *Poets & Writers*. Her other translations include María Ospina's short story collection *Variations on the Body*, *Reservoir Bitches* by Dahlia de la Cerda (nominee, International Booker Prize), *Recital of the Dark Verses* by Luis Felipe Fabre (winner, Queen Sofía of Spain Translation Prize), *Pink Slime* by Fernanda Trias, and *Comemadre* by Roque Larraquy (both nominated for the National Book Award in Translation), as well as a selected works of Oliverio Girondo titled *Poems to Read on a Streetcar*.